Marky, Slash & Levy: Return to Mavenwood

L.B. Fox

Illustrations by Nicole D. Bedwell

PublishAmerica
Baltimore

First printing

ISBN: 1-60563-350-X
PUBLISHED BY PUBLISHAMERICA, LLLP
www.publishamerica.com
Baltimore

Printed in the United States of America

Acknowledgments

Mark & Nick*: For being such outstanding models for my writing, you will always be the original Marky & Slash. Here's to good friends...*

Ethan*: Daddy loves you lots and lots!!*

Friends & Family*: To all of you who unselfishly supported me, you know who you are!*

Last, but not least, my thanks to ***God*** *for giving me a sequel through some tough times!*

Table of Contents

Chapter 1

Easy Times Inside the Birds Woods

As it rises, the light shines over three houses in the valley. All of the houses resided within a clearing in the woods to which grass grew flourishly. The house closest to woods was a stone house gray in color with a red brick roof that was very weathered but still strongly functional. The glass in the windows had a slight blue tint to them which mirrored reflections perfectly. On the side of the house rose a stone chimney with ominous purple smoke puffing out soft and gently. For inside this house, up a set of stone stairs leading to the third floor, one roomed attic. This attic was nothing more than a bedroom. With a wooden dresser drawer in one corner beside a window and a bed just on the other side, nestled into its own corner. Next to the window, in the stone wall was a brass hook, which seemed to be just as weathered as the roof over head yet just as useful.

On this hook hung a familiar object; the remaining piece of the Key of Briar, for this was the home of Marky.

Marky lay in his wooden framed bed under the covers quite comfortably and not to mention, warm. As the sun rose, all that could be seen was his nose. Marky, very much asleep, made no motion whatsoever except for his calm breathing underneath.

Now, the house in the middle of the three sat a stint farther back and rested at the bottom of the gently rolling hills that covered the Birds Woods.

This house was made of copper cobblestones all the way around and had large plank boards for the roof which had aged the color of the cobblestones. The crystal clear glass windows invited the eyes to see a well kept house inside with flowers growing in vases all over the living room. From the living room, rose a cobblestone stairwell up to the second floor of the home where three doors along the wall. It was at the end of the hallway where the door to Slash's room stood.

Inside Slash's room was a small bay window with a chest of drawers below and a steel framed bed with only a headboard. It was under the window inside the chest with the lid open; half of The Key of Lightning. The handle of the key and the chain were all that was stored under the lid of the chest. The sun shown into the room and it was clear the Slash was comfortable, with his feet sticking out from under the white fluffy sheets and his head, settled nicely into a feather stuffed pillow. Slash was sound asleep and appeared to remain that way for some time.

The third house in the clearing was the home of Levy. His home stood out in the clearing with only a single tree growing crookedly up beside it giving it complete shade. The home was made of large stones and tree branches that supported the upstairs. Inside the house over in the fireplace the wood glowed with a light hint of blue embers. In the corner of the living room underneath the hallway of the upstairs was a wooden door that led into Levy's room.

Levy had a small window which looked out over the clearing toward Marky and Slash's homes that were not far away. Levy too had a dresser drawer in one corner of his room but had a wooden nightstand beside his bed with a candle on it. Next to the candle, was remainder of The Key of Keen. The chain wrapped around the candle stick and looked as it had always belonged there.

Levy had a wood and stone bed built straight into the wall making it very strong but yet very comfortable thanks to the feather stuffed bedding that was placed inside. Under a thick homemade quilt, Levy was also fast asleep with his red and white striped tail hanging over the side of the bed.

As the sun rose into the morning sky, Levy awoke and crawled out of his bed and slowly walked out into his living room. Near by in the dinning room, a plate with oatmeal on it was gently steaming and ready to eat. Levy went to the table and sat down on his laurels and started in on his breakfast. After eating his breakfast, he took a few laps of clear water from a bowl beside his plate. He then he went for the door to go outside.

"You stay out of trouble, young man," said his mother's voice from the second floor.

"Yes Mother, I will," Levy replied.

Levy then opened the door and went outside. For the day seemed to be turning out to be quite wonderful and Levy decided he would spend it down at the pond.

Meanwhile, back at Slash's home, Slash was getting out of his bed to look out the window. He noticed Levy running across the clearing and obviously heading toward the pond that was near by. Slash noticed that his chest was open and closed it before heading down stairs to breakfast that was surely waiting for him.

Slash came out of his room and ran down the cobblestone stairway, which made a sound like two rocks being clicked together. Slash's favorite meal for his breakfast was toast which he approached. He quickly ate his toast and ran back up to the top of the stairs.

"I'm going outside for the day; I'll be with Levy mother," Slash hollered.

His mother hollered back, "That's fine, but you had best stay out of mischief today."

Out from the door in the middle of the hallway came Slash's mother, a white snow leopard with green eyes.

As Slash ran down the stairs, his mother stuck her head over the hallway railing and said as Slash reached the door, "Be on your best Slash, I saw Mr. Hanson the other day and he told me you and Marky had been over by his maple tree a week or so ago stirring up commotion again."

Slash stopped and looked up at his mother and cringed. Then just as quickly, he turned and opened the door and ran outside shouting, "Ok, mother, bye."

Out the door he when not quite pulling the door shut with his long black tail. As he was running toward the woods Marky was opening his door to step out into the day. He noticed Slash running by him at a galloping pace.

"Levy's at the pond," he shouted to Marky as he entered the woods.

Marky stuck his head back in and spoke loudly upstairs, "Father, Mother, I'm going to the pond, goodbye."

"Goodbye," his father's voice said.

"You be careful," said his mother.

With that said Marky closed the door behind him, and too, darted off toward the cool clear water of the Birds Pond for a day of excitement and fun.

Meanwhile, at the pond already, Levy was swimming about gingerly in the water. The water today was quite wonderful for swimming. The sun shown through the trees and warmed it just right for swimming. The wind gently blew through the trees creating a rustling sound of pure calmness. As Levy swam, all that that could be seen of him was part of his head and his tail, floating on top of the water.

It was not long before the pounding of Slash's quick feet could be heard, barreling toward the pond. Finally, Slash came into sight; he darted right up to the dock and out into the water making a moderate splash. Coming back up for air, he shook his head of water to clear his eyes.

"Wow," he said to Levy. "The water feels great today, and the sky, nothing but a little cloud or two."

"I know, it should be a good day for Canvass Sailing," said Levy.

"Yeah," said Slash poking his head back under water and then back up again. "Mother has my canvass patched for another go at the winds, it is as good as new."

Then came Marky in a gentle run up to the dock. He stopped at the beginning of the dock and walked to the edge.

"Well, fancy meeting you here," he said. "Mind if I add to the leisure?" he asked.

"Not at all, it is a perfect day for a swim," Levy said. "Jump in," he added.

"The water is great," hollered Slash.

Marky noticed his reflection in the water and noticed the small ripples on the surface. Finally with a rambunctious leap, jumped far out into the pond, greatly disturbing the small ripples. He rose up quickly and began his dog paddle out to the center where Slash and Levy had been.

"We're going to go Canvass Sailing today, do you want to join in?" Levy asked Marky as he approached them.

"That sounds great, I have been waiting to break in my new canvass my mother made," Marky answered.

"You have a new one, what does it look like?" asked Slash.

"It is red and has the picture of my key sewed onto it," Marky replied.

"Wow that really sounds like a great idea," Levy said. "Maybe I can get a picture of my key sewed onto mine as well."

The three swam around in the water for some time before going ashore and resting in the soft grasses lining the bank of the pond. With the wind blowing under the trees, it was hardly very long before they were completely dry and resting.

"You know speaking of keys," Marky said. "It's been almost a month since we have been to Mavenwood; I wonder what life is like there now without Zytor?"

"It has to be better than when we found it surly," Slash said while lying against a tree. "Maybe we should pay Randor a visit?"

"That sounds like a good idea; perhaps we can have a guided tour of the land without the dreadful events this go around," Levy said.

"Well, why don't we go tomorrow?" Marky asked. "I really would like to get some Canvass Sailing in today and show you my new canvass."

"Yeah that sounds great to me," said Slash.

"Alright," said Levy. "Today we should be able to get in some really good canvass time, which the wind is just right for."

With that said the three friends went back to lying in the grass. Each of them secretly laid thinking about their adventure just one month ago and how everything seemed to mean a lot more these days. After a while a strong gust blew through and Slash jumped up.

"Alright, I'm off to get my canvass, I bet I make it there first," he said.

Marky and Levy quickly got up and hurried off after Slash who was well on his way home to fetch his canvass.

Out in the middle of the clearing, back behind their homes, Marky, Slash and Levy were standing with rolled bundles of canvass beside them. They each grabbed the string wrapped around each one of their bundles. Slash opened his string and out popped the canvass which inside had small thin sticks that stretched out to form a solid frame. His piece of canvass had two patches on it that had previously been patched, suggesting that his canvass had won or lost some battles. The canvass, which was triangular, shaped was brown in color with green thread holding the patches together. At the end was a long white string for holding. With a gentle toggle, Slash hollered, "Ascend," to which the canvass took to the air and awaited command.

"Ready, how about you fellas?" Slash asked.

Levy untied his canvass, which unfolded into a diamond shape with thin green sticks framing the red canvass. Levy hollered, "Rise" and his canvass soared into the air, only stopping beside Slash's canvass as Levy held on by a strong blue string.

"Ok, I'm ready," Levy stated.

Marky leaned down and opened his canvas to show his friends just how wonderful it looked. As it unfolded, shiny silver rods formed the frame around the black canvass into the shape of a rectangle. With that beautiful embroidery depicting the Key of Briar on all four corners.

"Wow, that is quite something, look how new that is?" Slash said as he looked over Marky's canvass.

"Thanks, mother worked on it for several weeks," Marky said. "She had some trouble getting the framing sticks to fold out right."

"Well let's have it up in the air and have a go at it," Levy said to Marky.

"Climb," Marky said.

The canvass rose up to meet Slash and Levy's at a standstill, only to be stopped by the red string holding it to Marky.

"Ok ready?" asked Levy.

"Down to the tree line and back right?" asked Slash.

"Right, who ever makes it back to this point wins," Marky said to Slash and Levy.

They stood ready and took two steps forward and held on tightly as the canvasses in the air pulled the three friends hard across the clearing through the soft grasses and by lone trees scattered here and there. The canvasses seemed to race each other through the air pulling their owners.

Marky, who was in the lead, had a firm grip, but almost lost it when he came to a lone tree and had to jump out of the way to avoid being hit and thus, possibly losing. Slash meanwhile took advantage of Marky's misfortune and gained the lead over his friends. With no clear obstacle in his way he seemed sure to make it to the tree line first and start back to the beginning point. As Slash reached the tree line, he had trouble slowing his canvass and went into the woods just slightly, giving Levy the advantage. At the tree line Levy hollered "Around" which made the canvass turn effortlessly around right at the trees and race back toward the beginning point. Marky reached the tree line just as Slash was turning his canvass and coming out of the woods. Marky also said "Around" to make his canvass turn. He and Slash raced to catch up with Levy. Levy had a great lead over Marky, and Slash and it looked as if he would win the competition.

Marky hollered "Accelerate." This made his canvass speed quite rapidly. His canvass sped toward Levy quickly but Levy reached the beginning point just ahead of Marky, who was slightly ahead of Slash.

"Yes," said Levy. "Old fella still has it."

"You know best two out of three wins," said Marky. "This time let's see how fast the canvass will carry us."

"That a challenge?" asked Slash.

"It is a challenge," said Marky who turned to Levy. "Well, what do you say?"

"Alright, first one to lose control in the trade winds is out," Levy said.

"Fine," said Slash.

"Right," said Marky.

Marky put his paw over his canvass and commanded "Climb High," This forced the canvass high into the air, higher than before.

"You fellas had best hang on," Marky said.

Slash stretched his paw over his canvass and commanded "Ascend Upward," with that his canvass went higher than it had before. The high trade winds put his patched canvas to the test, yet it continued to hold.

"Levy, your turn, let's see what we've got," Slash said.

"Alright, here we go," Levy said as he too placed his paw over his canvass and hollered "Rise Upward." As fast as a bullet, levy's red and green diamond hit the air and was ready for competition.

"All ready?" asked Marky.

"Ready to go," said Slash

"All ready here," said Levy.

The three gripped their strings with their teeth and each one braced for the jolting start. The look in each others eyes was the same look that was seen on top of the Tower of Maytane.

"Ready, set," said Marky.

All at once the three friends shouted, (with strings in mouths), "Propel."

In a massive jolt, the Chosen Ones where pulled forcefully toward the woods at speeds faster than they had ever gone before while Canvass Sailing. They each struggled to hold onto their strings and did quite well being drug across the ground and all. As they reached the trees, they each began their turn. With the three in a dead heat they reached the woods. They each hollered "Around" however Marky's canvass turned and caught a branch at the top of a tree and became stuck. He knew that his part in the race was over. Slash and Levy executed their turns perfectly without anything blocking their way.

Slash and Levy raced back to the beginning point rapidly, so rapidly that Slash could not miss stepping on a rock and tripping and letting go of his string. Slash's canvass suddenly stopped overhead. Slash quickly jumped to his feet and grabbed his string and again was cast forward. However, Levy was gaining faster and faster until he reached the beginning point and one the race.

Slash flew in quickly across the beginning point to finish second. Meanwhile, Marky stood far down by the woods dealing with his canvass which was still stuck.

"I think we had better go see if we can help him," said Slash.

"Right, I would hate to see his canvass get torn, with it being so nice and all," Levy answered.

Slash and Levy ran across the open area toward Marky as he was trying to untangle his canvass. Slash and Levy's canvasses folded themselves up into small tight nit squares and awaited their return.

Once they reached Marky, he had one of the big tree branches cleared away.

"Is your canvass going to be alright?" asked Levy.

"Yes, it should be, I just had to clear this big branch so my canvass can close without tearing," Marky replied.

Marky, looked up into the tree and shouted "Collapse." The canvass folded itself just as Slash and Levy's had done. It fell toward the ground, however Marky was able to catch it before it hit.

"Well I think that is enough Canvass Sailing for today," said Slash.

"Right, those trade winds are fierce today," Marky said. "We're lucky we didn't tear any of them."

"What do you reckon we do now?" Slash asked.

"Why not take a trip down to Lawrence Hill and see what old Mr. Hanson is doing?" Levy asked. "It will give a chance to see what has been going on since the last time you two were that way."

"Alright, maybe he would like to hear about our adventure in Mavenwood?" Slash said.

"Of course," said Marky. "He loves a good story, and this time we can give him a good one indeed."

"Well then, let us each take or canvasses home and meet down by the tree line?" suggested Levy. "Then we can head that way."

"Good idea," said Marky. "I'll see you there."

"It won't take me long to get mine put away," hollered Slash as he ran for home.

The three friends each headed for home, Marky tucked his canvass under his bed. Slash placed his on a self near his bed. Levy placed his in the bottom drawer of his night stand. At the same time, as each of them was about to leave their room, Marky, Slash and Levy ran back in and grabbed their pieces of the Three Keys of Maytane. Marky snatched his from the hook on his wall. Slash reached for his out of his chest of drawers. Levy unwrapped his from around the candlestick and proceeded out the door.

Just as planned, Marky, Slash and Levy met at the tree line near the path that headed into the Birds Woods and to old Mr. Hanson, the owl who had a soft spot for the Chosen Ones, but never let it be known.

"Hey you brought your key?" Slash asked Marky.

"Yes, I thought it might make Mr. Hanson believe our story this time," Marky answered. "We have hard proof this time around."

"It is sometimes amazing to think of how we came to have these in the first place you know?" asked Levy. "I would have never thought it would be possible," He added as he held out his half of the key. Marky and Slash too held up their pieces; just then the familiar blue glow emitted from each key, only lighter than when they where first united but none the less glowed with unity.

"Look at that, isn't that wonderful?" asked Marky.

"It reminds me exactly how I felt when we came back home," Levy said.

"What a feeling right?" asked Slash to Marky and Levy.

As they let their keys down they ceased to glow.

"Well, let's take that feeling and go tell Mr. Hanson a story like he has never been told," said Levy.

The three then entered the Birds Woods on their way to visit and old friend.

Walking through the woods, they enjoyed the gentle warm breeze as it blew by into the Birds Woods. Things felt just a bit different than it had the last time they had been this far into the woods. Marky, Slash and Levy followed the same old wore path just as always toward the old Hackberry tree that Mr. Hanson had called home for as long as Marky, Slash and Levy had been alive.

Once at the tree, there sat Mr. Hanson, perched out on a limb with his back turned to the three friends. Now Marky, Slash and Levy had planned to announce themselves this time instead of jumping out in surprise, however Mr. Hanson could sense them.

"Well, if it the three young men who used to be children," Mr. Hanson said.

"How did you know it was us?" asked Slash. "We hardly made a sound."

Mr. Hanson turned his head to face the three friends.

"Because unlike the last time we talked, you each seem to have a mature presence about yourselves that was distinctively noticeable. As I look at you three, you seem to have a different air around you, might I ask why?" Mr. Hanson asked. "And where did you come across those remains of keys around here? I've never seen anything like those before."

"Well see that is just it," said Marky. "We have a story to tell you."

"Do you now?" Mr. Hanson asked curiously. "I am afraid I have heard all of your stories before so I am in great wonder what you have to tell me."

Levy began, "Well one day I found this large bone in the woods and fetched Marky and Slash to help me with the feast. When we got back to it, we began to dig to uncover it, hoping to pull it out and clean it a bit. But as we where digging we opened a large hole in the ground."

"A large hole you say?" asked Mr. Hanson. "Haven't heard this one before, go on please."

"Well," Marky continued. "We climbed down into the hole only to find a glowing green river flowing right out of solid rock. We followed the river into a large cave and that is where we met our new friend Reamy; a bat who guarded the cave. He then led us out into large woods unlike anything in the Birds Woods. The trees talked and Randor, the second oldest tree there told us that we were expected."

"Really, and what was it that you were expected for?" asked Mr. Hanson jokingly.

Slash jumped in, "To save this strange world of course. We were chosen to defeat an evil lord who was causing turmoil all over. We were asked to defend it, and we did just that."

Slash jumped into the air.

"We crossed prairies, climbed hills," Slash said.

"Don't forget the falls," Marky mentioned.

"Right," Slash continued, "We fell from this mythical falls, crossed an eerie bridge with killer fish and..."

"We fought evil wreaths, dark ghosts, crossed a white desert, and much more," Levy added.

"Please continue," said Mr. Hanson with growing interest in the originality of the new story.

Marky gladly continued, "There was the earthquake in Hindoes that Slash almost did not make it through."

"And the stairs that Marky almost fell off of," added Slash.

"Along with the hot air in Hyden," Levy said. "We saw the most colorful birds you have ever seen, killer roots that came out of the ground. And the muddy marsh of the Wabasha Valley was horrible to cross."

"But we had to get ahead of the Dry Icers," Slash said.

"Dry, Dry Icers?" asked Mr. Hanson.

"Yes, they where the evil clouds that chased us all over Mavenwood," Marky said.

"Mavenwood?" Mr. Hanson asked again.

Levy replied, "That was the world we where in. Go ahead," he told Marky.

"We met a lot of bad thing in that world. We met the Dark Shadow which almost turned us all into stone before Slash saved us. Then, there were the fish that attacked us on the Boundary River while we tried to cross that eerie Cretan Bridge."

"Wow that sounds like a lot of bad things was there any good things?" Mr. Hanson asked.

Slash answered Mr. Hanson, "Oh Yes, we met Nelty who is a very very good friend who helped us get to Tormor, and Crete, who saved us from the Dry Icers, Then their was Ebeneezer, Artimus, Mutter, Latos, and of course Reamy, Randor, and Hamel."

"Then there was Grainger, quite the odd man out wouldn't you say?" Marky said.

"Yeah" Slash said.

"I still can't shake that cold mysterious feeling that I had when he appeared." Marky answered.

"Why was that?" asked Mr. Hanson.

"Well see," said Levy. "He was this green little worf, like a troll, that appeared out of thin air, told us how to Marky's key and then just as quickly and silently vanished again."

"Key?" Mr. Hanson questioned.

"The Three Keys of Maytane that we had to use to defeat Zytor with," Marky said as he showed Mr. Hanson the Key of Briar.

"But your keys, they are broken?" Mr. Hanson wondered out loud.

"That is how Slash sealed the Triangle of Holding while Marky and I were hurt," said Levy.

Mr. Hanson seemed confused.

"Zytor, the evil lord destroying Mavenwood was using an evil cyclone to destroy towns and valleys," Marky said. "The keys close the Triangle of Holding and entombed the cyclone forever."

"And the evil lord, how did he meet his end?" asked Mr. Hanson.

"He was blasted into Embarrass River where he melted in the thick blue water," Slash said proudly.

"Then we were given much praise and sent home, and then the next day after we each awoke we found the remaining pieces of our keys lying on our beds," Marky said.

"Wow, now that was some story," Mr. Hanson said. "That truly bests all of the others."

"But it is true as life itself," said Marky as he began walking up to Mr. Hanson. "You must believe us."

"Marky, Slash, Levy, it was a good story," Mr. Hanson said.

"Slash, let us show him," said Levy.

"Right," Slash answered.

Slash and Levy walked up to Marky and touched their keys to his which gave off the light blue glow.

Mr. Hanson's eyes grew very wide with disbelief.

"That, that really hap happened?" he asked.

"Yes sir," Marky, Slash and Levy all said at the exact same time.

"Well, I'll be, that explains the change in your presence," Mr. Hanson said.

"Our presence?" asked Slash.

"I couldn't quite place it until you told me your story," said Mr. Hanson. "Your fascinating adventure has changed you more than you realize."

"Yes?" asked Marky.

"You three are far more confident and understanding about yourselves and the things around you; in fact this is the first time the feathers on the back of my wings did not puff up," said Mr. Hanson.

After a long pause of silence, Levy suggested they get back home. The three friends said goodbye to Mr. Hanson and began their walk home. For the first time, Mr. Hanson had a smile on his face as he watched Marky, Slash and Levy walk away.

"Good lads," he said.

As for Marky, Slash and Levy, they each were thinking hard about what Mr. Hanson had said. Such admirable words coming from someone as wise as Mr. Hanson send an even bigger sense of pride through each of them.

As night fell Levy sat in his room staring at the Key of Keen and began to think about tomorrow and seeing some friends he hadn't seen in a while. A knock at the door pulled his attention away, and he got off of his bed and walked across his living room where his mother was putting a log onto the fire making it burn a deep dark purple.

"Are you getting that?" asked his mother.

"Yes mother, I know that knock at our door," Levy answered.

He walked over to the door and pulled on the wooden handle and opened the door. It was Slash at the door standing in the dark with only the light from an outside door candle burning.

"Slash, what are you doing out at this time of night?" Levy asked.

"I thought I might stay over," Slash answered. "That way we can leave at the same time together."

"Oh hello Slash," said Levy's mother, who got up and walked to the door. As she walked up she said, "Leave together, do you have a big day tomorrow?"

"Uh, yes, we are uh...," Levy said.

"Uh, we're going to Kelso Creek tomorrow and caught some Yellow Belly," Slash jumped in and said.

"Oh, well you just be careful, that is a ways there and is at the edge of Birds Woods," Levy's mother said. "Is Marky not going with you, that is quite strange?" she asked.

"No mother, he is going with us we will just meet up with him tomorrow," answered Levy.

Levy no more than had the chance to finish when Marky came around the dark corner of the house and stepped into the light of the candle.

"Hello," he said. "Nice night isn't it?" he asked.

"Hello, Marky," said Levy's mother. "Are you going to Kelso Creek tomorrow also?"

Marky looked at Slash and Levy inside the house shaking their heads yes. He looked back to Levy's mother and answered.

"Yes mam, were gonna catch Yellow Belly." He said quickly looking at Slash and Levy for approval. Slash and Levy blew a sigh of relief.

"Mother, is it alright for Marky and Slash to stay over tonight?" Levy asked.

"Yes," she said. "But remember to fetch some Cypra Wood for the fire pile before your father and brother return from their trip."

Marky walked in and walked over to Levy as he shut the door behind himself.

"Where have your father and brother gone?" he asked.

"They went to Knox to sell Ginger Weed at the market there, Scray begged father to take him," answered Levy.

"So you're in charge then?" asked Slash.

"Only for a while, they will return in a day or so after father has sold all of the Ginger Weed," Levy said.

"Or until Scray begs to come home," Marky said. "I'm sure tomorrow Klin will be over here searching for him."

"Oh I'm sure Klin knows already that Scray has gone Marky," said Levy's mother, who was preparing the kitchen to end the night.

"Well let's turn into my room for the night, goodnight mother," said Levy.

"Good night boys, don't forget about the Cypra Wood Levy," said Levy's mother.

"I won't mother," Levy answered.

Marky, Slash and Levy entered Levy's room and closed the door, there they sat until the candle had almost burnt down to nothing talking about returning to Mavenwood and how they would enjoy the time there, and by the time the candle had burnt completely out, the three friends where fast asleep, Levy on his bed and Marky and Slash on thick rolled out rugs on the floor.

As the long night passed soon it was day.

Chapter 2

The Return of Marky, Slash and Levy

With the morning light shining through his bedroom window, Levy awoke to find the day outside somewhat cloudy, looking as though it might rain by days end. He climbed out of bed and woke Marky, and Slash.

"Fellas, wake up, it's mid morning," Levy said.

Marky and Slash woke and looked outside the window as they each stood up and stretched. Levy began to make his bed while Marky and Slash rolled up their rugs and placed them under the bed.

"Well, that should be it, " said Slash.

The three friends walked passed the kitchen to find three place settings of ground oatmeal made on the table with three bowls of milk. A note lay beside the place setting in front of Levy's chair from his mother that read: 'I have gone into Birds Woods to fetch more oats have fun today.'

"Wow, Levy," said Slash. "Your mother always knows when you going to be up, even when it's late."

"I know," Levy replied. "She says that she can sense when I am going to wake up just by hearing through the door." Sitting down the letter, he continued, "She's gone into the woods to fetch more oats so she will not be here to see us off."

"Well, let's eat," Slash said with a hungry stare. "It smells wonderful."

Levy pulled out his wooden chair and sat down at the table. Marky too pulled out the chair next to him and sat down and sipped some milk. Slash pulled out Scray's chair and sat down and began to eat the oatmeal. The three ate slowly and enjoyed their breakfast thoroughly, until they were full. When finished, they each got up and placed their dishes unto the sink. Levy pulled a string next to the sink, this allowed warm soapy water to flow from the faucet and fill the sink. The sink quickly filled as the water began to bubble and the dishes moved around cleaning themselves.

"There," Levy said. "When there done mother will put them away for us." He turned toward Marky and Slash and asked, "All ready?"

"I think were all set." Marky answered.

"Well let's be on our way then," Slash happily said.

Marky, Slash and Levy left the house and headed toward the Birds Woods down a path that was barely traveled. The wind blew warm again today just as it had yesterday but blew softer through the treetops. They followed the old path a good ways into the woods. Before they knew it, they had come upon a familiar object. The large bone that had started their adventure stuck out clear as day laying next to a large tree with roots that stretched out for several feet. This tree stood over a hundred feet tall with long thick branches stretching out quite far. Marky, Slash and Levy walked up and stopped.

"I had forgotten all about that bone," Slash said. "I don't believe it's still here."

"I've been keeping it safe for you," said the tree in a soft tone.

"Hello, Hamel how have you been?" asked Levy.

"Very good," Hamel answered. "It seems like forever since we last spoke does it not?" he asked.

"Yes, it does seem like a long while," Levy answered. "I apologize for the time away."

"After what you have done for us, there is never a need for apology," Hamel answered back.

"We would like to return to Mavenwood for a visit," Marky said. "However the hole has disappeared."

True, the hole that they had uncovered seemed to have vanished and, in fact, never existed.

"Allow me to help you with that," said Hamel.

Hamel pulled back a section of his roots to uncover the entrance to Creek Cave. This time, the feeling of curiosity they felt when they had discovered the hole was now replaced by the feeling of excitement.

"When ever you wish to enter all you must do is ask," Hamel said. "Now run along and enjoy your visit."

"Yes, we will," Marky said.

"Well, after you," Levy told Marky and Slash.

Marky walked up to the hole to find stairs leading down into Creek Cave. This suited him better than before when there was nothing to do but jump into the hole. Followed by Slash, Marky hurried to the bottom of the stairs.

"Thank you for keeping this a secret," Levy told Hamel.

"I shall guard this opening for you," Hamel said. "I will close it behind you to insure its safety and yours. Now, down you go."

"Alright, I'll be going," Levy said who went down the stairs and joined his friends.

As promised, Hamel closed the opening behind them just as before. When back to normal, it looked as nothing had ever existed.

Now inside, Marky, Slash and Levy were back at the Creek Cave. The River of Guidence glowing green, gave them the light they needed to make it through the cavern. Again the river waves followed them at the pace they were walking. Levy walked over to the edge of the rock pathway they were walking to the riverside. He knelt down and touched the water.

"Thank you very much for your help," he said. "Without it I'm afraid we wouldn't have made it."

The water's waves dispersed and clamed for a moment and then rippled again, it would seem, as if to be replying.

"Let's keep on ahead," said Marky. "Perhaps we will find Reamy hanging up a ways."

Marky, Slash and Levy continued on as did the River Of Guidence down Creek Cave until they once again entered the large cavern that Reamy called home. They looked all over and found no sign of Reamy. As they looked over the ceiling of the cavern, Reamy entered from ahead.

"Hello, my friends, I trust your visit will last a small while?" Reamy asked as he flew in to the three friends. "I apologize for not being here to greet you; I have been helping Randor with the apple harvest for your visit."

"You knew we were coming?" asked Slash. "How?"

"The Book of Knowledge said that the Chosen Ones would remain true friends and return many times." Reamy replied.

"We apologize for not returning sooner," Levy said.

"It is alright, you needed to regain your strength from your last visit to Mavenwood," Reamy said.

Reamy then flew down to Marky, Slash and Levy and perched on his feet.

"If you will follow me, I will take you to Randor," Reamy said.

"That would be great," Slash said. "Is that where you have the apples, the last ones were delicious."

"Yes they are there, waiting for you," Reamy replied. "If you wish I will take you into the Woods of Syrus now."

"Yes," Marky answered. "I think it is safe to say that we are quite ready to see the woods in a relaxing tone."

Reamy then flew forward into the cave ahead that led toward the Woods of Syrus. Marky, Slash and Levy followed. Soon, they reached the end of the Creek Cave and were standing at the foot of the woods.

From the edge of Creek Cave, you could see the wind gently blowing through the trees. The three friends stood for a moment and stared at what they had helped to protect. A sense of pride could be felt inside each of them.

"Well friends," said Reamy. "If you will follow me, Randor will surely be happy to see you have returned."

Marky, Slash and Levy followed Reamy in the Woods of Syrus. Once they came under the canopy of its leaves, the cool crisp air welcomed them as it blew past. It seemed as though nothing had changed, however this visit to be one of conversation and enjoyment.

"Is Randor around?" asked Levy.

"Yes, he attending to business on the boundary with the Godway Region but should not be gone for too much longer I reckon," Reamy replied.

"Well then it should not be a problem for us to wait then?" Marky pondered.

As they reached a familiar clearing in the woods, Reamy stopped and perched on a tree limb that was close to the ground.

"Since you three have left, there has been a great many changes," Reamy began. "The Scats have begun to expand their village further out into Hyden now that there is no threat of Zytor of attacking. The Crackers have begun to let outsiders into the Falls of Euphoria, saying they no longer fear the location to be in such danger. The Scats are also planning to build a bridge across the Boundary River. And there is even talk of a unified reconstruction of Tormor."

"All of this has happened since we left?" asked Slash. "Things move awfully fast here."

Reamy replied, "You forget that our timetable moves quite faster than your own, in your world you have only been gone but a few seconds."

"I'm sorry," said Slash. "That's something I have to get used to down here."

"How is it possible that a unified reconstruction of Tormor is possible?" asked Marky. "How does something like that take place?"

"Well, the Collective Council handles issues of worldly impact," said Reamy

"The Collective Council?" asked Levy.

"Yes, they are made of members from six regions of our world, who work as a collective unit when issues of world effect take place," Reamy stated. "They are the ones who decided to open the Creek Gate that led you here before."

"Why was we not told about them before now?" asked Slash.

"As Zytor's deconstruction grew, the council agreed to break way to avoid being targeted as well." Reamy continued, "Randor thought it best to consult the Book of Knowledge, which called for you three as the only hope to defeat him, Randor leads the council and decided to open the gate. They broke away after that decision, but have since rejoined in discussion of Tormor."

"Wow, how often do they meet?" asked Marky.

"I am glad to hear friendly voices asking questions again." said Randor, who was coming back from his business.

"Randor," Levy said as he, Marky and Slash hurriedly walked over to greet him.

"It is good to see you Randor," Marky said.

"It has been a while but we are glad to be back to visit," Slash said with a smile.

"I have been sure that you would return on a calmer setting to enjoy and converse," said Randor.

"We are sorry for taking so long," said Marky. "It was such an adventure that we needed time to take in all that we had done."

"We more than understand," Randor explained. "You are most celebrated; I suppose one would need a moment to recollect."

Then Slash spoke up.

"Reamy was telling us all that has been happening in Mavenwood since we left. Is it true that Tormor is going to be rebuilt?" he asked.

"We have been discussing Tormor's future. Word has gotten out that there were a handful of Tormites that escaped Zytor and fled into the Godway Region to safety. It is the belief of the Collective Council that these few should have a home to return to, and since there is so few of them, we have been discussing collectively reconstructing the ruins."

"That sounds like a massive undertaking?" asked Levy.

"It is somewhat complex," Randor explained. "However, all that is needed to rebuild anything is Construction Powder, and in Tormor's situation, several bags of it."

"Construction Powder?" asked Marky. "How does it work?"

"Construction Powder restores any object it is spread on back to its original form according to its glorious prime," Randor answered.

"And all it takes is enough powder to cover Tormor to restore all that was destroyed?" Slash asked.

"Yes, when that time arrives it is my hope that you will be here to see the process in its motion," Randor said.

"Well what can we do to start our visit with so many sights to see?" Slash asked.

"How's about a celebration?" Reamy mentioned.

"A celebration is a wonderful suggestion to welcome the return of the Chosen Ones," Randor proclaimed. "Let us begin a celebration." he said while waving his branches into the air and running toward the other trees in the woods.

Then several of the trees in the Woods of Syrus came to life and began to move around lighting lanterns and gathering apples from the orchards here and there. It would not be very long until dozens of lanterns were lit and apples overflowed the grounds of the celebration. Reamy, Randor and the other trees of the forest joined in to create a wonderful celebration of food and music, which was created by the trees blowing on branches with holes created like flutes. The music was very fine and echoed through the Woods of Syrus like light across the ground. Soon the two suns in the sky had set and the lanterns flashed light through the trees as Marky, Slash and Levy ate and sat to enjoy the festivities.

Randor stood still also enjoying the music with a smile on his face and with Reamy perched on one of his lower limbs.

"It is quite nice to hear the music echo through the woods again, does it not?" Randor asked Reamy.

"Yes it is a wonderful sounds to hear once again," He answered. "Thanks to the Chosen Ones, we have the opportunity to hear this for a long time to come."

Randor and Reamy looked down to Marky, Slash and Levy who watching some trees slowly dance in circles in joy.

"This is one of the greatest things I have ever been a part of," Slash said.

"I know," Marky said. "It is such a wonderful break from home."

"I have never heard music so joyous and clear to the ear," Levy said. "It is incredible, all of this," he added.

Then from off in the distance, a small group of brush began to stir and shake. The noise caught the attention of Marky, Slash and Levy. They stared quite interestingly at what ever might come through the brush. Reamy and Randor too were waiting in order to see what would appear.

The noise and movement suddenly stopped and nothing could be heard but the crackling fire from nearby.

Then without warning a skinny gray troll jumped out from the brush. The gray troll had black marks all over its body. It had no hair and bright blue eyes. Its attire was nothing more than a cave man style gown. It stood almost five feet tall but could hardly stand because it was breathing so heavily that the opportunity to stand upright did not present itself.

Marky, Slash and Levy jump and backed toward Randor and Reamy, unsure what this strange looking troll had appeared for.

"What is it?" asked Marky.

Reamy flew down to Marky, Slash and Levy as Randor walked closer to the gray and black troll, who could hardly move, due to its heavy breathing.

"I don't believe it," Randor said.

"Yes Randor?" asked Levy.

"It appears to be a Powder Troll from the Land of Nothing." Randor said. "They have not been seen past the Tapa River for many years."

"Does it mean us harm Randor?" asked Slash.

"No," Randor answered. "They are a shy creature. I am curious as to what drove this one so far away."

Marky then noticed that the troll had something in its hand.

"It appears to be holding onto something," he said.

As the troll lay down, for lack of breath, Levy walked over to it and nudged its hand. The troll opened its hand as a chunk of stone fell out. Levy picked up the chunk of stone and looked it over. He noticed that there appeared to be lines carved into it, however, he could not make anything out.

"Randor," Levy said. "What do you make of this?" he asked as he held up the stone.

Reamy grabbed the stone and flew up and dropped in into the palm of Randor's branch. Randor looked the stone over carefully and took a deep breath.

"Randor is everything alright?" asked Marky.

"I do not believe what I see, could this be...," he asked himself.

Reamy perched on Randor and observed the stone for himself.

"That cannot be," He said.

"Do you know what this is?" asked Levy.

"This cannot be," Randor said.

As Marky, Slash and Levy looked on Reamy spoke while still looking at the stone, as if still not believing it was before them.

"Is this a piece of the Stone of Afadavis?" Reamy asked.

"If it is then that can only mean the legend not foretold in the Book of Knowledge is true," Randor said.

"What legend is that?" asked Marky.

As Randor held the small piece of stone he began to explain himself.

"It is mere legend, but the Stone of Afadavis is said to be the key that is supposed to unlock a device so powerful that it could destroy anything in its path," he said.

"Can it destroy like the Dark Plague of Tormor?" Asked Levy.

"I am afraid that this device is far more power than the Dark Plague of Tormor could ever be," Randor answered. "I have heard that this device could level one fourth of our world with one blast."

"Where does this device exist? Slash asked.

"No one knows, this has always been legend, no one has ever seen this device, no one that has ever been recorded," Randor answered.

Reamy then spoke out.

"But if this piece of stone is in fact a piece of the Stone of Afadavis, than the legend must be correct, and this threat must be real," he said.

"Who would want to find this stone now that Zytor is gone?" asked Levy.

"I am afraid I do not know that either," Randor said. "This is the first time we have ever had a situation arrive that the Book of Knowledge could not explain. However…," he added.

"Yes?" Marky questioned.

"There is someone who might know," Randor answered. "I shall wait until tomorrow to venture to the border and visit him."

Marky, Slash and Levy each looked at each other for a moment and each shook their heads. Marky looked up at Randor and offered to help.

"Randor, we would like to help if we can," he said.

"My friends, I am afraid that this time I cannot enlist your help," Randor said.

"I am sorry, but why is that?" asked Slash.

"With, the Book of Knowledge saying very little about this catastrophic device, I cannot foresee your safety or danger," Randor replied. "I appreciate your help but I would fear for your well being."

"Randor," Levy said. "If you don't mind, we came close to our own deaths to save this world and we won't let another chance such as that to happen again."

Randor replied, "But this time you are not the Chosen Ones, you can't know what might happen or where this journey may lead."

"Still the same," Marky answered back. "We surely didn't save this world just for it to come to an end some time later. We want to help."

"In a way, our last adventure made us feel like we were a part of this world," Slash said with pride.

"We won't return home until this is finished," Levy said.

Reamy walked over closer to Randor and whispered.

"Their motivation is pure, maybe they could help find this device if it does lay somewhere in our world," he said.

Randor looked at Marky, Slash and Levy and thought for a moment about the situation. Marky, Slash and Levy stood waiting for his answer. Randor then shook his head in agreement.

"Very well, tomorrow we shall venture to the border and find some answers about this stone," Randor said.

"And for the Powder Troll?" asked Reamy.

"See to it that he is soaked in the River of Guidence and allowed to revive on his own, perhaps he can tell us what he has seen," Randor answered. "For now it is best to rest for the journey, it is a good distance to the border of the Godway Region. Our destination is the Great Wall of Marketstan."

The celebration ended and after a short while, all where resting for the evening.

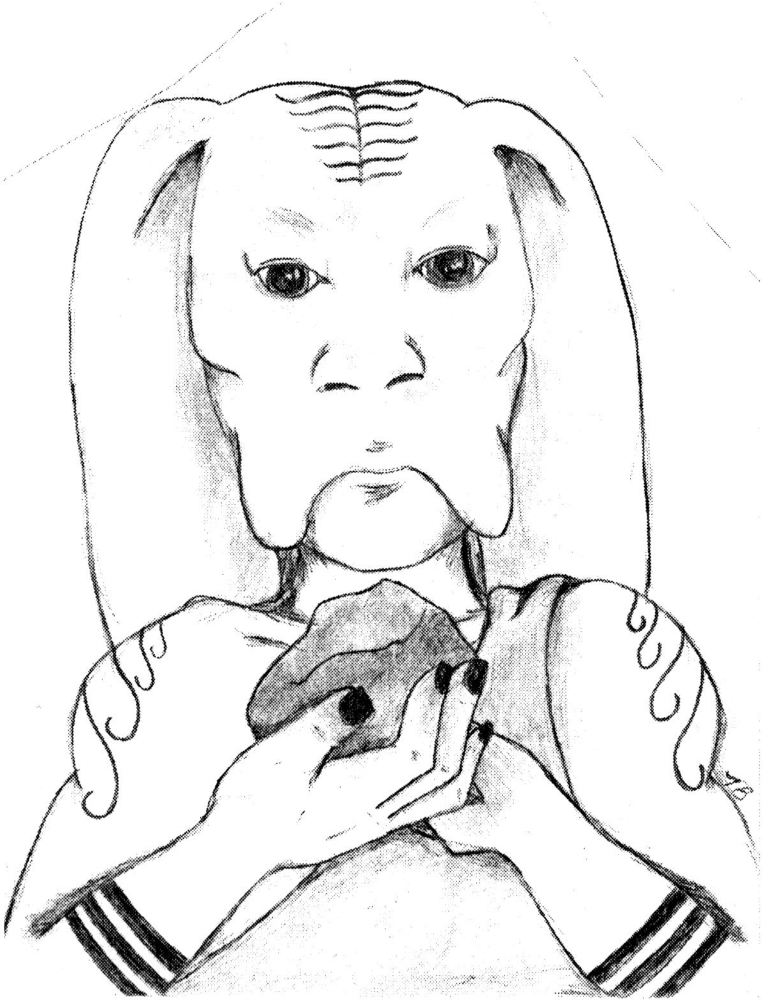

Chapter 3

The Great Wall of Marketstan

When the morning light began to shine through the Woods of Syrus, Marky, Slash and Levy woke to a peaceful calm breeze blowing through the trees and a soft tune being sung by pink crows in the tree tops.

Marky, Slash and Levy each stood up and looked around to find no one near. They began to look around in hopes of finding anybody.

"Where is everybody?" asked Slash.

"Surely Randor would not leave without us," Marky said as he began looking off into the woods.

"No," Levy said looking around behind him. "Randor would keep his word."

"Well, should we look down by the River of Guidance?" Slash asked looking in the direction of the river.

"Yes, perhaps they are tending to the Powder Troll," Marky said. "We might find out how he is doing."

The three began down the path toward the River of Guidance until they came to the glowing green river flowing in a calm soothing manner. They walked up to the bank of the river only to look around and find no one around.

"No one is here," Slash stated.

"Surely, no one has gone," said Marky.

Then, from behind, Randor's voice called out.

"I see you have awakened my friends," he said.

Randor was sitting at a large wooden desk made from old logs and bark. On top of the desk sat many large books, different in color but all with gold binding. On the corner of the desk sat a quill inside an ink bottle. The quill was a feather, red in color with black strips inside.

"We thought we had been left behind, Randor" Marky said. "I apologize for assuming that."

"Have no worries about your confusion," Randor answered back. "Reamy has gone to inform the Collective Council of our finding and report on our journey."

"But who will be guarding Creek Cave?" asked Slash.

"The cave has been temporarily sealed until his return and shall be under the watch of the Guards of Syrus," Randor answered again.

"When will we be leave for the Great Wall of Marketstan?" Levy asked Randor.

"We will leave shortly," Randor replied. "I am waiting for the Powder Troll to revive from the river."

"So there has been no contact with him yet?" asked Slash.

"I am afraid that this troll had come many miles before reaching us," Randor stated. "When he begins to wake, we shall bring him ashore to dry. Reamy will be back by then and will be able to talk to him and find any information he might know."

"It will be worth knowing where he came across that stone, if in fact it is a piece of the Stone of Afadavis," Levy said.

"I am quite curious as to how he came to bare it," Randor wondered out loud.

Just then, the Powder Troll began to cough, which rippled the waters of the river. Although he was very weak, he was able to grasp the shore and hold on. Marky, Slash, Levy and Randor went over to him. Randor then reached down into the water and scooped up the gray and black troll from the glowing waters of the River of Guidence and carried him onto the shore a ways before laying him to rest in the grass of the woods.

As Randor stretched him out, into a comfortable position he spoke.

"There, you shall be fine after some time," he said, "You will be quite comfortable here until you are able to stand."

The troll lay still, except for moments when it would shake ever so slightly and turn its head from side to side. After a moment the shaking stopped and its body remained still, to do nothing but breathe. Randor stood back upright and looked to Marky, Slash and Levy.

"Our new friend will be just fine here until Reamy returns from the council," he said. "If you are still full enough we will begin our journey toward the Great Wall of Marketstan, there we will find the answers we seek."

Marky, Slash looked at Levy and shook there heads. Levy then answered Randor.

"We are ready Randor," he said.

"It is a far reach to the Godway Border but we shall make it there in good time," Randor said. "If you wish, you may travel on my branches."

"I think we would like to start out the journey on foot for a ways first," Marky said. "But will be sure to keep up."

Randor smiled at the three friends and turned and headed into the woods.

"That is the spirit that calms my emotions," he laughed.

Marky, Slash and Levy followed Randor in line as they set out toward the Great Wall of Marketstan. As they walked away, the Powder Troll remained still as if sleeping in the grass.

It would not be long into the journey that the, once again, three travelers were seeing the Woods of Syrus by means of a time important journey. As they walked, the warm, calm winds blew through the trees that stood so still in the daylight, as if they were resting from the past evenings celebration. The sky light shown through, making the woods shimmer with dancing light for as far as anyone could see.

"This woods is huge, how long would it take to cross it, from one side to the other?" asked Slash.

"If we were to start at this time and head across the Woods of Syrus, we would end up on the other side in one day in your world," Randor replied.

"So in Mavenwood it would take about a five turns of the skylight?" asked Marky.

"I am beginning to understand why you were the Chosen Ones," Randor said.

"You understand?" asked Levy.

"Yes, you three are far more intelligent than you give yourselves credit for," Randor answered.

"Randor," asked Marky. "What is it we seek at the Great Wall of Marketstan?"

Randor answered, "The Great Wall of Marketstan is home of Gecko the Great. He will be able to tell us about this piece of stone."

"Who is Gecko the Great?" Levy questioned.

"Gecko the Great is the oldest living creature in Mavenwood," Randor said. "He is mentioned in the Book of Knowledge, almost at the very beginning. He was one of the founding members of the Collective Council. He has been less noticeable these days, but will have answers to our questions."

"Is the Godway Region home to his people?" Marky asked.

"He has no people," Randor replied.

"He is all alone?" asked Levy.

After walking a ways, Randor answered Levy.

"Gecko the Great is the last of his kind," he said. "The Waffers died out because they were unable to evolve any further into the future."

Marky, Slash and Levy attempted to understand Randor's story. Each one inside felt sympathy for the Waffer they had yet to meet.

This feeling made them feel a sense of pride in knowing that they had each other.

Overhead, Marky, Slash and Levy heard the wind blowing through the leaves creating a hollow and ominous sound of music. The music aided their journey by giving, if only briefly, a sense of peace and happiness in sightseeing.

After some time of traveling, Randor stopped and sunk his roots into the ground to soak up the minerals for his meal.

"Let us stop for a moment and gather our energy back," he said.

Randor then sprouted apples from his branches and dropped them to Marky, Slash and Levy. As they sat and began to eat Slash was surprised.

"No matter how often we eat these, they taste just as good as they did when we first tried them." he said. "Syrus Apples have a changing taste element inside them, which make them taste remarkable no matter how many times one eats them."

The shiny red apples looked so clean and refreshing that the three friends could not help but be sure to eat their fair share of them. The more they ate, the more comfortable they made themselves in order to enjoy their brief stop.

Marky sat next to a large clump of dark green grass rubbing his right ear against them. Slash sat by Randor licking his paws after his meal. Meanwhile Levy looked through the Woods of Syrus, simply enjoying the view of the massive trees rooted in the gently rolling hills, which created a wonderful sight in the light.

"Randor," Slash asked. "How much farther is the Great Wall of Marketstan from here?"

"We are no closer than half way," he replied. Then he continued, "When we come close to the Godway Region, we will see the high, flat lands that make up the terrain. Gecko the Great resides inside the great wall much like a cave dweller."

"Will he know we are coming?" Marky asked, pulling away from the grass.

"No, but he always welcomes a member of the Collective Council into his cave," said Randor.

With that said Randor pulled up his roots from the ground and stretched out far and wide. With a big yawn, Marky, Slash and Levy stood up and each too stretched and prepared to continue onward.

"We should continue on our way now my friends," Randor said.

Randor turned to began again with Marky, Slash and Levy close behind.

Meanwhile, back at the River of Guidence, Reamy returns from his meeting with the Collective Council and begins to oversee the Powder Troll lying in the grass, motionless. Reamy flies over to Randor's desk and grabs inside a small open shelf under the desk and pulls out a tear drop shaped bottle with a glass cork in it. Inside this green bottle was a bright blue liquid which sloshed around until Reamy sat it into the desk.

Reamy then flew down to the grass and broke a blade of grass from the roots and carried it back to the green tear drop bottle. Then, he dipped the blade of grass into the bottle and coated the end of the grass with the blue liquid. With the coated grass, Reamy flew down to the Powder Troll and with a quick but gentle flick of his wing, flung the blue liquid onto the troll.

After a few moments of breathing, the troll began to move its fingers and toes. Although it did not open its eyes, Reamy could see the troll's eyes moving under its eyelids.

"There my friend," he said. "Just a little Tinsel Liquid should help aid in your awakening. You should wake up quite soon."

Reamy sat quite puzzled at the Powder Troll. He slowly walked back and forth thinking in his mind about the image of the stone that was brought into the Woods of Syrus. As he looked at the troll Reamy noticed that there was a small scare on the right side of its back. This made him wonder how the troll had gotten it.

"My poor friend, how in my mind did you come up with that scar?" Reamy asked.

By now the troll had almost dried completely and appeared a much brighter shade of gray then first thought. The black stripes wrapped the troll in a spiral pattern from the back of its neck down to its left foot. This intrigued Reamy, as he had not seen a Powder Troll for many, many years.

As Reamy watched over the Powder Troll, Marky, Slash, Levy and Randor grew closer to the boundary of the Godway Region. The landscape of the woods now became increasingly hillier and had deep valleys. Still the four pressed on with determination to find Gecko the Great.

"Good news my friends," Randor said. "We are nearing the Godway Region. After we reach the border, it will not be far inside before we reach Gecko the Great."

"Randor, you say that he welcomes all members of the Collective Council into his lair, will he welcome us inside as well?" asked Levy.

"You will be more welcome than even I," Randor answered. "You are the Chosen Ones; he will take to you most warmly. Gecko the Great will surely find you three most interesting."

"That is good news," said Slash. "The weather looks cloudy; at least we won't be left out in the weather if it decides to turn bad."

Marky, Slash and Levy followed Randor for a ways longer. Having walked a great distance in a short time the three where somewhat worn out, however they continued onward.

Randor stopped at the top of a very steep hill. As Marky, Slash and Levy reached the top; they too saw what Randor saw. Before them was a region of enormous canyons and extremely deep valleys. This region was adorn with hundreds of mountain high plateaus that were flat at the top and covered with nothing but a handful of large rocks place here and there.

"We have reached the Godway Region," Randor said.

"This view is spectacular," Marky said. "I've never seen anything like this."

"There is a small pathway that leads us to the Great Wall of Marketstan," Randor said. "Once we reach the wall, we shall see the home of Gecko the Great."

Slash looked down the other side of the hill top and was shocked to see how far it was to the bottom.

"I can hardly see the ground below," he said. "How far down is that?"

"We have no way of knowing," Randor replied. "No one that has ever ventured down into the bottoms has ever returned to tell. When we reach the wall, it is very important that you not fall off the side of the path."

Levy stepped forward and looked around the area.

"We had better be going, I am interested in knowing what it is that we have," he said.

"Yes," Randor agreed. "If this is one of the pieces to the Stone of Afadavis, then time may be a resource we don't have."

The four continued forward along the tree line of the Woods of Syrus passing the tall trees to one side and far drop on the other.

"You will do fine," One tree said as they passed by.

Slash looked at the trees but saw no movement by any of them.

"Do not fear Gecko the Great," said another

"He will point you in the way needed," spoke yet another.

As Marky, Slash and Levy looked around at the trees they could see no movement. However they did take comfort in the encouragement they had received from the trees.

To their left the steep sloping hillside had turned in an almost straight drop down. Below the ground could hardly be seen through a gentle covering of clouds. Levy could see a river flowing far below but not much more than that. All that could be seen out across the horizon, which was setting, was miles and miles of large canyons and deep valleys.

"I would take forever to cross this area," Marky said.

"Until someone does cross it and make it back we will never know," Randor said.

Slash and Levy continued to watch the pathway ahead, which narrowed shortly as they came around a corner.

"Be careful," Levy told Slash. "We can't afford to fall."

"That sure is a long way down," Slash replied.

Randor then stopped after seeing their destination. As Marky, Slash and Levy stopped, Randor spoke.

"There it is, the home of Gecko the Great," he said.

As Marky, Slash and Levy looked around Randor, they could see the Great Wall of Marketstan, which looked much like the wall outside of Creek Cave. There was a cave carved into the wall with a large red cloth like canopy draped over the front to block the weather. There was a lone tree growing from the outside. The tree looked like the type growing inside the Woods of Hationstare. At the base of the tree was a dirty yellow flag with a star on it waving in a gentle breeze. On the wall itself, on both sides of the cave opening two torches burned to welcome the night.

"We will be most welcomed," said Randor.

Randor than began to move toward the cave. After observing the large wall up close, Marky, Slash and Levy ran quickly to catch up with him.

As they came around the bend in the path, the Woods of Syrus on the right, gave way to a rock protrusion that Marky, Slash and Levy their sides to in effort not to far into the Godway Region. Now with the Great Wall of Marketstan on three of their four sides, the wind blew very strong and very hard in a circular motion as it crashed into the wall.

"I can't hold on much longer," Slash hollered. "The wind is…so strong."

Levy, who was digging his paws into the ground with all his might moved closer to Slash and placed his head against Slashes side in effort to hold him back.

"You can make it, it is not much further," Marky said to Slash.

"Stay close to me," Randor said. "The path widens ahead."

Soon the wind began to die down. As the path widened, the wind calmed to a small breeze. Randor stretched his branches to strengthen his leaves. Marky, Slash and Levy each shook to calm the hair on their bodies.

"Here it is," Randor proclaimed.

Marky, Slash and Levy looked up to see the entrance to Gecko the Great's lair standing before them.

"The lair of Gecko the Great," Randor said. "Come my friends, for inside lay our answers."

Randor curved some of his branches downward so that he could fit into the cave. He walked slowly under the cloth like canopy as to not tear it. Marky, Slash and Levy each entered behind him.

Several feet into the cave, was a large red curtain. This curtain was very large and looked to be extremely heavy. As the four approached it, the curtain drew back from both ends and allowed them through.

"I guess we are expected?" Marky asked out loud.

"Yes, this is the sign of welcome ness," Randor answered back.

"How far into the cave does Gecko the Great live?" asked Levy.

"Not far," Randor replied.

Past the curtain were blue flamed torched that lit the cave up to a solid stone wall.

"Alright, how do we go past this," asked Slash.

Randor then waved his branch hand across the stone wall and spoke:

"Acumulas artania," he said.

The stone wall began to disappear in the middle in the shape of the cave entrance. Soon the rock had completely disappeared, leaving an opening into a large room filled with maps, books, globes, compasses and large magnifying lenses on stands.

The lit torches illuminated the large room showing the large ceiling with a chandelier made of four torches hung down. Torches also hung on the walls above each of the seven bookcases that were against the walls. As the blue flames burned, Randor called out.

"We've come to speak with Gecko the Great," he said.

No replied answered back. Marky, Slash and Levy were surprised with the lack of sound inside this new room. All that could be heard was the blue torches burning.

"Perhaps we have missed him," Levy said aloud.

"Surely he will come back soon," Slash said.

"Well," said Marky. "We have to solve the mystery of this stone, so we must wait for his return…right Randor?"

"Do not assume that just because you cannot see something that it is not there at all," Randor replied.

With that said Marky, Slash and Levy first looked at each other and then began to call out.

Marky said, "Hello…is anyone here?"

Slash called out, "We've come seeking answers to our question."

Levy then spoke, "May we speak with Gecko the Great?"

Just then a book on a desk in front of the four, across the room turned one page as a voice spoke: "Randor how nice it is to see you."

Then a creature began to appear out of nowhere from behind the book. This creature was brown in color, with a large robe on that glimmered in the torchlight. The robe was made of every color imaginable, as was the pointed hat on his head that a yellow rope emerged from the point. The creature also had a small button nose with two whiskers on each side and long ears that stuck up quite far.

An old pair of wire rimed glassed were on his face, as if to help him see. These glasses wrapped around its ears. Marky, Slash and Levy noticed the creature push these glasses up on its face several times while climbing a ladder to put the book back on the top self of the middle shelf.

"I am glad you have stopped by for a visit," The creature said. "It has been a while."

"Yes it has been a long while," Randor said.

"Not since Zytor unleashed that menace onto our world," said the creature climbing back down the ladder.

As the creature reach the bottom of the ladder and turned around, he looked through his glasses and noticed Marky, Slash and Levy. He then hurried toward them.

"I'm sorry, who are you?" the creature asked.

"These are the Chosen Ones," Randor said.

The creature then looked Marky, Slash and Levy over quite carefully in pride.

"So," he said. "You are the ones who defeated Zytor at the Tower of Maytane?"

Levy then answered, "Yes sir, we are the ones."

The creature continued to observe the Chosen Ones.

"Fine strong willed lads you are," he said.

"We've come looking for Gecko the Great, would you be able to tell us where he is?" Slash asked.

"If you have come looking for Gecko the Great, then look no farther," said the creature.

"You are Gecko the Great?" asked Slash.

"That is right, I am who you are here to find," said the creature.

"I am afraid this is no general visit," Randor said.

"No?" Gecko the Great asked.

"We have something we must have you look at," Randor said.

Randor then handed Gecko the Great the stone found by the Powder Troll. Gecko the Great then hurried over to one of the three large magnifying lenses that were on wooden stands near the torches in the ceiling. He placed the stone under the lens.

"Hmm...yes it is stone," Gecko the Great said.

He turned the stone and observed some faint markings on one side. Gecko the Great read what he could, then he raised his head from the lens in shock.

"Where did you find this?" he asked looking at Randor.

"A Powder Troll from Land of Nothing stumbled into the Woods of Syrus with it in his hand," Randor said.

"Did this Powder Troll tell you anything about how he came upon this?" Gecko the Great asked.

"He became unconscious after turning over the stone," Marky said.

"Do you know what this is?" asked Levy.

Gecko the great looked at Randor and then back to Marky, Slash and Levy. He then took a deep breath and answered.

"This mark says, Loomis," said Gecko the Great. "Loomis is a word in the Airtime language means attack from the air."

"Airtime?" Slash asked Gecko the Great.

Randor turned to Slash and answered his question.

"Airtime is the language of the Clan of the Clouds, a race long since gone from Mavenwood," he said.

"What happen to them?" asked Levy.

Gecko the Great answered, "No one knows what happened the Clan of the Clouds. They are mentioned far back into the history of our world. Back farther than I have even been here," he continued. "They once lived in our world both on land and in the sky where they created their civilization before coming down to us."

"How long ago did they disappear?" asked Marky.

Randor answered, "They disappeared about one million of your years ago."

"Why does their disappearance have attachment to the stone?" Levy asked.

Gecko the Great answered, "It is rumored that their civilization as a whole, were the original guardians of Mavenwood. It is also rumored that they created something in order to defend our world."

He then held up the stone.

"This piece of stone is a part of a larger stone that is supposed to be the key to that very protection. However, this key was supposedly shattered by the Clan of the Clouds just before their disappearance.

The fact that this Powder Troll found it and brought it into the Woods of Syrus and turned it over to you makes me wonder how it found it and why it felt it necessary to get rid of it."

"Could someone else want this piece?" Marky asked.

"If that were the possibility, and this device was used for evil, then it could destroy the world with a force that would dwarf the Dark Plague of Tormor." Randor said.

Marky, Slash and Levy stood in awe of the thought of this things power.

"The Clan of the Clouds called this defender the Doomsday Device," said Gecko the Great.

The room fell silent again with only the sound of the blue torches burning. After a long silence Randor spoke to Gecko the Great.

"Is there a way to find the other pieces?" he asked.

Gecko the Great walked over to his ladder which was hooked to a sliding pole that allowed it to roll from bookshelf to bookshelf. He then pushed it to the far side of the room and began to climb.

"There may be one way to find the rest of the stone since the Powder Troll is unable to tell you anything," he said.

He then reached at the top of the bookshelf and grabbed a large, very dusty old book in the corner. As he climbed down the dust fell off of the book like powder. He then walked over to one of the large lenses again and carefully placed the book on the ledge underneath and carefully opened it. As Gecko the Great opened the book, the spin cracked and popped.

"This book is the Book of Legend; in here one may find answers to anything not found inside the Book of Knowledge," he said. "I am sure we shall have your question answered, Randor."

As Gecko the Great peered into the large magnifying lens, Marky, Slash and Levy drew in quite close to observe. As he turned the pages, the three friends could see that the book was written in a language that they could not read. There were many pictures of strange and magical creatures and large battles in the old days of Mavenwood.

"This book looks very old," said Levy.

"Yes, it is older than I," Gecko the Great said. "I found this book while I was on a scout in Nightvania. I can only assume that it was created by the first to walk this world."

Then Gecko the Great turned to a page that read 'Treimel Hartis.'

"Here it is," he said.

"What does Treimel Hartis mean?" asked Slash.

"It means Doomsday Device," Gecko the Great replied.

He then turned the page and began to read.

"The Clan of the Clouds built the Doomsday Device as a weapon of peace. It was meant to protect the regions of Mavenwood by simple means of protection. The power of this weapon was so great that no creature on Mavenwood dared to attempt an attack for fear of their own destruction. Mavenwood lasted in peace for many thousands of years."

He then turned the page. The next page showed a drawing of the large round stone being broken into six pieces and scattering all over the map of Mavenwood.

"However," Gecko the Great said. "Before the Clan of the Clouds disappearance, they broke the stone into six pieces and scattered them over Mavenwood, Look." he said as he pointed to the small piece in the picture and then to the one in his hand. "This is the smallest piece of the six. The other five pieces are large and more in danger of being found if just one of them is discovered."

"How can that be?" asked Randor. "Is there a connection between the pieces?" he asked.

Gecko the Great answered, "By collecting one of the larger pieces, one will be led to each of the pieces in the order that they were broken off."

"So then we can find where the other pieces are with this one also?" Marky asked.

"I am afraid not young friend," responded Gecko the Great, "This piece is the last of the whole stone to be touched, it will not link you to the rest of the stones because has no stone after it to connect with."

"How will we find the first piece of the stone then without a guide to it?" as Levy.

Gecko the Great turned the next page and read the strange language aloud.

"I need to stop evil, the good must travel to the Tower of Maytane, only there will the guardian of the tower decide the worth of the takers," he read.

"The Tower of Maytane?" asked Marky. "That's where we sealed the Dark Plague of Tormor."

"You must go to the Tower of Maytane and stand before Rago; there he will decide whether or not to give you the first piece of the Stone of Afadavis," said Gecko the Great.

"So it is all true," Randor said. "If someone is seeking that stone and indeed plans to use it, then we have no choice but to take the journey to the Wabasha Valley and recover the first piece of the stone."

"You must be very careful," said Gecko the Great. "I cannot begin to tell you how difficult the road will be or where the road will lead you but you have my hopes."

Randor the looked at Marky, Slash and Levy and leaned over to them.

"You three travel back to the Woods of Syrus and inform Reamy of our information and situation while I go to the Tower of Maytane and recover the first piece of stone," he said.

The three friends looked at each other with the same determinate look that they had when accepting the journey toward the Triangle of Holding. For each of them were thinking the exact same thought.

"Randor," Levy said as he stepped forward. "We would like to be the ones to go to the Tower of Maytane. We can reach it much faster and I feel that time is in small supply."

With that said Marky and Slash walked up behind Levy with the same looks on their faces.

"My dear friends, you are so brave," Randor said. "If you take this journey you will have to be on your best wits and alert."

"We will bring get the first piece and bring all of the pieces back before anyone can use them," said Marky.

"Well then," said Gecko the Great said as he walked over to a red round bottle sitting on a ledge along the wall by the entrance. "Take this as my effort to keep you all safe."

He then reached inside the bottle and cast the red powder across Marky, Slash and Levy.

"This is Soul Dust; it will help reduce the strain on your bodies and will give you more energy for what I feel will be a long journey," Gecko the Great said.

As the dust settled on Marky, Slash and Levy, it disappeared.

"Now be on your way," Gecko the Great said. "May time be on your side."

Marky, Slash and Levy turned and walked back toward the curtain. Again, the curtain rose in front of them.

"Wait outside for me, I shall be along." Randor said.

"Alright Randor," Levy said.

The three walked into the cave as the curtain closed behind them.

"Randor," Gecko the Great.

"They are brave souls; I believe that their bond together will be the difference," Randor said.

"I trust their unity," Gecko the great announced.

He walked with Randor to the curtain and stopped as the curtain rose.

"If we are unsuccessful in finding all of the pieces, you must approach the Collective Council and advise them. I fear that if someone is to operate this legendary device, they must know as soon as possible," Gecko the Great continued. "Now old friend, see to it that our friends are sent on their way with safety."

"I have learned to trust in their safety, they are quite strong," Randor said.

Gecko the Great shook his head and Randor walked through the curtain. After the curtain closed Gecko the great then spoke quietly to himself.

"May luck be on our side," he said.

Gecko the Great then disappeared in the room.

Meanwhile, outside the cave, standing in the blowing wind, Marky, Slash and Levy were gathered waiting for Randor. The wind was cool as the sky light had now gone and the night light had set in. Shadows appeared all around, thanks to the blue torches burning strongly.

"Another adventure huh?" asked Marky.

"Yes," Slash answered. "But we have done this once before, I believe we can do it again."

"Levy?" asked Slash. "Do you believe we can do it one more time?"

"I've got a feeling," he answered Slash.

"What do you feel?" asked Marky, who walked closer to the group.

"I feel that this journey is going to be one that will take quite some time to complete," said Levy.

"Longer than before?" asked Marky.

"Much longer," Levy replied.

Marky and Slash looked at each other and then back toward Levy.

"But I know we can see this through," he said.

"That's what I had hoped to hear you say about this journey," Randor said coming out of the cave. "I believe your desire to keep this world safe is what makes you each of you courageous."

"So I suppose this is where we go in separate directions now?" Slash asked.

"To reach the Tower of Maytane, you must continue on this pathway, down along the Godway Region," Randor said. "You must stay on the path and not fall into the Godway Region, I fear that if you fall, you may never return. The path will then cross the high lands of the region by means of Sikes Bridge; however the bridge is quit worn so you must watch your footing. The bridge will lead you to the boundary with the Wabasha Valley, travel straight and you will come to the Aqua Bridge which crosses the Embarrass River. From there, you will head straight toward the tower and stand before Rago."

"And when we recover the first stone?" asked Marky.

"Return to the Woods of Syrus and we shall present it to the Collective Council," Randor directed. "I wish to leave the last piece with the council to safeguard from uniting the stones under evil hands."

"As soon as we find the stone we will return," Levy said.

"Then may luck and time walk hand and hand on our quest," Randor said.

"It will Randor," Slash said with a half smile.

"Then now I leave you to retrieve the first stone and I will tend to our new troll friend," Randor said. "I expect he has awoken by now and will be able to tell us how and where he came across the first piece."

"And the last stone, what who shall carry that?" asked Levy.

Randor answered, "I feel that it will be safer on the move with you than in one place with me."

"We forgot the stone inside," Slash said.

"Just because you did not see the exchange does not mean it did not happen," Randor said. "I expected Gecko the Great to keep it but on the way out, he had placed it in my side to carry out. I feel that he too wishes it not to be in one place for to long."

"But how will we carry the stone?" asked Levy. "We have no means to carry it with us."

Randor then pulled out the stone and held it in his hand.

"I will aid you as much as possible with any burden," Randor explained.

Then with a wave of his other branch hand over the stone, the stone began to glow bright yellow and with a flash of bright light, the stone had become incased inside a chest harness with the stone in the center. The harness made a criss cross pattern with the stone secured tightly.

Randor reached down to Slash and placed the harness around his head and neck. Slash then stepped into a strap that went under his chest.

"Me?" asked Slash.

"You are the quickest and most nimble, you will best protect the stone" Randor said. "That is why I entrust it to you. Now you three be on your way, I will return to Reamy and look on the Powder Troll."

Randor turned and began to head back down the path which the four had come over.

"Well, we best get going," Levy said.

The three friends then turned and began to follow the path ahead further into the Godway Region.

Meanwhile, in the Woods of Syrus, Reamy sat perched on the desk by the river resting from his travel. He opened his eyes when he heard the movement of the Powder Troll in the grass. The troll was beginning to awaken and move ever so slowly to stretch.

Reamy flew down to the troll to greet it when its eyes opened. Finally, the troll slowly opened its eyes and looked around. When seeing Reamy the troll quickly opened his eyes fully and jumped to his feet.

"The stone, where is the stone?" the troll asked Reamy.

"Fear not, for it is in safe hands," Reamy answered.

"The stone must not fall into the wrong hands," said the troll.

"So the stone is in danger?" Reamy asked.

"You know of the stone?" asked the troll.

"We have wondered, but some friends have gone to seek answers," Reamy said.

"Is it protected?" Asked the troll.

"Yes, quite," Reamy answered.

The troll then calmed down and sat down on a rock near the waters edge. Reamy flew back to the desk and perched calmly.

"What is your name?" He asked.

"Kelso, my name is Kelso," said the troll.

"Can you tell us where you came across that piece of stone?" asked Reamy.

"Well," said Kelso. "I am from the Land of Nothing, where my kind live in peace and harmony on the flatlands. One day as some of us were out picking Celp, the Chiller came from nowhere and forced us into short term slavery. We were made to dig in places near the center of our land. We were told to look for a rough cut stone in the black dirt and bring it to him as soon as found. I remember overhearing him say that as soon as they had the smaller piece they would begin the search for the remaining pieces with the two that they had."

"They?" Reamy asked. "There was more than one?"

"Oh yes," Kelso answered. "There was only the one Chiller, but he commanded hundreds of Mirrormites from the Dark Valley."

"Mirrormites?" Reamy said in shock. "Hundreds of them?"

"The more we dug, the more frustrated he became," Kelso continued. "He complained about the stone being to small to locate exactly and that time was being wasted."

"That was when you found the piece, wasn't it?" Reamy asked.

"Yes," Kelso answered. "When I uncovered the stone, I knew that it would be in dangerous hands had I turned it over. So I ran far away from my home and headed toward the Woods of Syrus where I heard that Randor of the Collective Council lived. I have heard that the Book of Knowledge might tell of this stone and it might be safe."

"Well," Reamy said. "It was wise of you to bring it here; Randor has in fact seen the stone. He and some friends have gone to ask Gecko the Great for answers. They have been gone since early morning light. I do not expect them to return until morning light again, it is a strong walk to see him."

"Would you tell me the importance of this stone?" asked Kelso.

Reamy flew down from the desk and walked over to Kelso and attempted to calm him more.

"I think it is best to wait until Randor and our friends return with answers before we worry."

"I am not even sure that this piece is deserving of worry," Reamy said. "However, hundreds of Mirrormites gathered under control of someone other than their own needs enough to worry."

Reamy paused for a moment and changed the subject.

"Until Randor returns let us eat and rest for the remainder of time," he said.

Reamy and Kelso decided to walk into the woods to eat before Randor's return. Although it was dark outside, Reamy could since the surrounding and Kelso took advantage of the night light. It was Reamy's hope that food might calm Kelso down.

Chapter 4

Close Encounters

With the sky light creeping over the horizon, Marky, Slash and Levy are very careful not to fall off of the small trail.

"We have to be getting closer," Slash said.

"We have no way of knowing," Levy said.

"Randor must not have known how far it would be for us," Marky said.

"Does the ground seem to be getting closer?" Slash asked.

Marky and Levy looked at the ground far below. The clouds covering was not as hazy, however the ground did not seem any closer to them.

"I am afraid that we're no closer to the ground than we were when we first saw it," Levy answered.

"Well, we know at least that it will begin to get closer once we come to Sikes Bridge," Marky said.

The three carried on with the path hugging the Great Wall of Marketstan ever so closely.

A many days journey to the other side of Mavenwood, in the flat black dirt ground covering the Land of Nothing (a land of black ground spotted with short pink leaved trees bearing a red berry), a Mirrormite (a tall black troll like creature with white antlers and a beaver-like tail) walked in a hurry toward a clearing, stepping over the small Powder Trolls. Once in the clearing he addressed a figure that could not be seen due to a small Dwarfwood Tree blocking the figure.

"Yes?" the figure asked.

"Sir, you are correct, the Powder Trolls have still not uncovered the piece of stone," he said. "What will you have us do?"

"Send out the Sky Crossers in the direction of the skylight; tell them to search for the troll who has escaped with the stone," the figure said.

"Escaped sir?" asked the Mirrormite.

"I have reason to believe that the smallest piece of the stone is getting farther away even as we speak," the figure said.

"As you wish sir," the Mirrormite said before he turned to leave.

"My dear troll, where are you going with my stone?" asked the figure.

Although the figure behind the tree was not visible, something else was visible. Beside this figure laid a larger piece of the Stone of Afadavis. The corner of this piece was glowing a white beam of light on the edge in the direction of the ever rising sky light. This light was directing the figure in the direction of the smaller piece.

Just as this was happening, back across Mavenwood in the Godway Region, Marky, Slash and Levy continued to walk the narrow path along the Great Wall of Marketstan. The path is widening, however the three friends must still walk in single file. As they walk Slash kicks some loose pebbles off the side of the path and watched them fall far down to the ground below.

"Be careful," Marky said. "We can't get too close to the edge."

"I know, but I have never been up so high and been able to see down," Slash said.

Levy was looking up at the Great Wall of Marketstan; the rack wall went up another two or three miles higher.

"Imagine if you were up there," Levy told Slash.

Slash looked up the wall and was breathless as he looked up the scaling wall. As Slash looked up the wall, he began to lose sense of where he was going. He began to wonder away from the wall with notice. Slash then slipped, he went quickly over the side. Levy then leaped to grab Slash before he lost his grip. Marky, hearing the noise turned and reached for Levy before he too would go over.

"Hold on," Levy told Slash as he used his front paw that was free to push himself back up the side of the wall.

With Marky grabbing on to Levy and Levy grabbing Slash by the scruff of his neck, helped pull Slash back onto the path to safety. With Slash catching his breath he thanked his friends.

"Thank you," he said. "I can't believe I walked away from the wall."

"The important thing is that we are alright," Levy said.

"That's right," Marky said.

The three friends took a momentary break to catch their breaths and then stood up and continued walking. Off in the distance Marky could see, what to him looked like a bridge ahead.

"I think I see Sikes Bridge ahead," he said.

They continued onward for a good while with the bridge becoming closer with every step.

Once they reached Sikes Bridge, Marky, Slash and Levy stood looking at the old, worn down bridge.

"That's Sikes Bridge?" asked Slash.

"It must be because the path turns and crosses the bridge," Marky said.

"Then we cross it," Levy said.

The bridge was much wider which allowed Marky, Slash and Levy to walk side by side as they stepped out onto the bridge. The bridge before them stretched farther than they could see ahead. Sikes Bridge was very straight but off in the distance it was clear that the bridge slowly curved and headed toward the Wabasha Valley.

The bridge made cracking stone sounds from underneath. Dust and powder fell from the underside of the orange stone bridge which arched from one plateau to another out across the Godway Region. Still Marky, Slash and Levy pressed onward.

"What is that sound?" asked Slash.

"It is just the bridge supporting our weight," Marky said.

"That does not sound much like support," Slash said.

"Don't worry, I have a feeling that it will hold for the length of the journey," Levy said back.

Sikes Bridge was covered in dust which left light footprints on the bricks that made the bridge. Every sixty or seventy steps, on both sides, where pedestals that held lanterns which had long since burned out. Small bricks composed the bridge and the lanterns looked to have been once made of very polished brass.

"It feels nice to have some room to walk," Marky said.

"With the journey taking us a good ways on this bridge, that is a good thing," Slash said.

"At least we know that the Wabasha Valley is at the end of this bridge," Levy said.

"It sure will be strange to see that tower again after what happen there," Marky said. "I never thought that we would see it again, at least not so soon."

"But we must go to the Tower of Maytane one more time, so that we can protect Mavenwood," Levy said.

Marky, Slash and Levy pressed on, no realizing that far off into the distance, that something was heading toward them, the Sky Crossers.

Back in the Woods of Syrus, Reamy and Kelso sat in a clearing inside the woods talking about the stone while waiting for Randor's return.

"How did you know to come to the Woods of Syrus?" Reamy asked.

"It is widely known that Randor was the most noble of the Collective Council and that he possessed the Book of Knowledge." Kelso answered. "I knew that if I could make it to the Woods of Syrus, I could give the stone to him and that it would be kept out of evil hands."

"This creature who wanted it, what is he like?" asked Reamy.

"He walks with a cursed air about him," Kelso replied. "It is like his soul is overwhelmed with the search for these other pieces."

Then off in the distance Reamy could here Randor approaching. He flew up into one of the trees and listened closely.

"Randor approaches," Reamy told Kelso.

"These other friends you speak of, are they from the Collective Council also?" Kelso asked.

"No, these friends come to us from another world," Reamy replied. "They were the Chosen Ones who cleared our world of Zytor some time ago."

"The Chosen Ones," Kelso said with amazement.

"Yes, they are the friends who have gone with Randor to Gecko the Great," Reamy said. "However the sound I hear does not include their footsteps."

"You are correct in what you hear." Randor said as he stepped into the clearing. "Our friends are not returning with me, but rather are heading towards the Tower of Maytane in search of the first piece of the stone."

"So then it its true?" asked Reamy. "It is a piece of the Stone of Afadavis?"

"That is correct, they are going to retrieve the first piece of the stone and then bring it back to us," Randor said.

"Back here?" asked Kelso.

"Yes," said Randor. "It was very brave of you to bring us the last piece of the stone. What is your name, new friend?"

"My name is Kelso," he said. "It is an honor to meet you Randor."

"Shall we wait for them then?" asked Reamy.

"Yes," replied Randor. "The first piece will guide us to the next pieces in order in which they were broken off."

"Oh no, that is not good," Kelso said.

"What troubles you Kelso?" Reamy asked.

"If that is true then the Chiller will be led here by the stone that he possesses," Kelso said.

"What, another has a piece of the stone?" Randor asked.

"Yes, the one who forced us to dig for the stone which you have," Kelso said

"Then it is very important that they not carry both pieces with them back here," Randor said. "For if they bring them back here and they are joined with this other piece then this other creature will be able to find the remaining pieces and activate the Doomsday Device."

"Randor, what shall we do?" Reamy asked.

"We must try and reach the Tower of Maytane in time to stop them from bringing both pieces back here," Randor said.

With that Randor, Reamy and Kelso began their trek toward Marky, Slash and Levy.

As they headed toward the Wabasha Valley, Marky, Slash and Levy too where headed in the same direction. Still on Sikes Bridge, Marky, Slash and Levy were being very cautious not to disrupt the bridge.

"Look far ahead," Marky said. "The Embarrass River, we're not far from the end now."

Marky was right, for far ahead the Embarrass River; flowing with crystal splendor and grace.

"It feels as if we have been walking on this bridge forever," Slash said.

"Do you feel that?" asked Levy, who stopped on the bridge.

"What?" asked Marky.

"I don't feel anything," Slash replied.

"The air is changing," Levy stated.

Marky stopped and surveyed the sky around them but saw nothing to cause alarm.

"I can't see anything; the sky appears to be safe," he said.

"Maybe your right," Levy said. "Perhaps it is nothing."

"Well we had best be on our way," Marky said.

The three friends then carried onward, however only a few dozen steps later, Levy again stopped and tried to understand the feeling he was sensing.

"What is it?" Slash asked.

"Something feels wrong," Levy answered back.

"What is it?" Marky asked.

Marky and Slash walked over to their friend and stood near the edge of the bridge. Although the thought of falling through weighed heavily on their minds, the fact that Levy was having this feeling again had their foremost concern. They stood staring into the sky which shown very brightly now thanks to the sky light. Levy, with his ears pointed highly, listened to the wind as it slowly passed by. Then, Marky had a sensation pass across his nose.

"Wait, something smells different now," he said.

"What is it?" Slash asked while looking all around.

With his nose in the air he replied, "Smells musty, I can't quite place it."

Slash then turned to Levy.

"Anything?" he asked.

Levy listened very carefully before replying.

"It is faint but it sounds a lot like a wining noise, it is getting louder," he said.

Marky, Slash and Levy then walked right up the side wall of the bridge and intently looked, listened and smelled. As Slash stared out into the sky, he noticed a dark blue speck in the air getting bigger as it approached.

"I see something," Slash said.

"Can you tell what it is?" Levy asked.

"No, not yet," Slash answered. "But whatever it is, it is getting closer."

"That is where the noise is coming from," Levy said as he backed away from the side wall. "Something doesn't feel right about this. I think we need to get off of this bridge."

Marky and Slash quickly backed away from the side wall as well. Without exchanging any words, the three took off running as fast as they could toward the Embarrass River and the end of the bridge.

The blue mass in the sky gained on them, closer and closer. Soon it was clear what this thing looked like. The blue figure was in fact an evil looking creature who rode upon a dark blue dragon of the same color. The figure was very tall and looked like a knight, but no good night. It wore a dark blue suit of armor with an insignia of a cracked sun on the chest. On its side was a sword with the handle of a two headed dragon on the end. On its shoulders, were blue metal guards wrapped with a metal braid of briars crossing them. A metal helmet covered the head with another braid of briars circling the head as a shard of metal shot out of the center toward the back of the head gear. The only glimpse the helmet gave of the creature beneath was the white eyes that burned through the helmet like fire.

It rode toward Marky, Slash and Levy on a dragon with a long pointed tail and with claws that were so long, it looked as if the dragon could reach down from the clouds and touch anything it so wished. It flew through the air with large wings that cut the air in two. White mist blew from its nose as it pierced the sky.

Meanwhile, at the edge of the Land of Nothing, a Mirrormite guard rode up to its leader with news from abroad.

"The Sky Crossers were dispatched earlier but have yet to report," he said. "I suspect that it will be some time before we hear of any news."

The leader still could not be seen but from just ahead of the Mirrormite guard, spoke to his soldier.

"Fear not, for they shall return news and perhaps even the small stone," he said. "In the mean time we shall hold up our forces until we hear word."

"Yes sir," the guard said as he turned and walked away.

Back again at Sikes Bridge, the Sky Crosser began to dive down toward the bridge as it closed in on Marky, Slash and Levy. They turned around in time to see clearly what was heading for them.

"It's coming," Slash hollered.

The three ran harder. Slash, being the fastest, was far ahead with Levy and Marky following behind. The Sky Crosser swooped down and made a grab for Marky. Marky however leaped to the road below and missed the claws of the dragon as they scrapped across the bricks, stirring up dust. It flew high up into the air as it made a turn and began to come back down.

"It's coming back," Marky hollered as he started to get back up.

This time, the Sky Crosser headed for Levy who was running his hardest behind Slash. Levy stopped when he heard Marky yelling. Just then the dragon made a grab for Levy. Levy leaped toward the side wall just in time to miss the dragon's claws reaching for him. However the leap was so sudden and hard that Levy leaped to far past the side wall and almost went clear over the edge of the bridge. Fortunately, Levy was able to grab the side of the bridge and hold on.

This left Slash who had slowed to see about his friends.

"Go," Marky yelled as he headed toward Levy.

Slash again sped up to elude the Sky Crosser. In Slash's favor was his speed. He pulled away from the Sky Crosser as he neared the Embarrass River. The Sky Crosser then shook the reigns of the dragon and the dragon quickly flew ahead of him. Slash continued to run seeing the Sky Crosser coming for him.

The Sky Crosser could see the small stone piece strapped to Slash's chest. It knew that it wanted the stone and had closed in, so that it could grab the stone away. Slash then had an idea. He continued to run until the dragon was upon him. He quickly stopped short of the dragon, which crashed into the bridge. The bridge almost instantly gave way and the Sky Crosser and dragon fell through. The smashed bricks fell into the river with large splashes. However, before the Sky Crosser would hit the river, he pulled back on the reigns of the dragon and flew back upward, but as he flew the dragon let out a horrible cry as it had a torn wing thanks to the bridge.

Once back above the bridge the Sky Crosser decided that it was wise to return with the news of the stone, rather than risk more injury to his dragon. With a brief stop to stare at Marky, who was still heading toward Levy, Slash, who was staring back, and Levy who was pulling himself back over the side wall, he flew away. Slash stared until the creature had almost disappeared. Marky and Levy soon joined him in staring.

"What was that?" asked Marky.

"I have no idea, but I don't see it returning anytime soon," Levy answered.

"It wanted the stone didn't it?" asked Slash.

The three then turned to look at the bridge before them. The Sky Crosser left little to cross but a single row of bricks of the right side wall. Marky, Slash and Levy walked up to the edge of the bridge and looked down to the Embarrass River which flowed like nothing had disturbed it. They then looked at the single row of bricks and walked toward them.

"We need to cross one at a time," Marky said as he climbed onto the side wall and slowly creped across the river.

As he crossed the dust fell from the bricks. Once across he dared to stand and await his friends.

Next Slash climbed upon the edge and hurried across the bricks. Once on the other side he walked past Marky a ways to ensure that the bridge would not be over burdened.

"It looks as though it will hold," Slash hollered to Levy.

Levy climbed back onto the side wall and greeted the air below him.

"Hello again," he said.

With several sly moves, Levy quickly moved across the bricks and reached the other side.

"That was close," Marky said.

"Let us hurry into the Wabasha Valley and retrieve the first stone," Levy said.

"Then we take it to Randor." Slash said.

With that, Marky, Slash and Levy began the downward slant of Sikes Bridge into the Wabasha Valley. The bridge made a gentle slope down into the valley. The three only had to walk for a little ways before reaching the end of the bridge. Once at the end, they noticed the bridge ran almost into the ground as the ground turn into the marsh like ground that covered the Wabasha Valley.

Levy noticed at the end of the bridge the sidewalls formed two small pillars with engraved pictures of two creatures with cloaks completely covering them except for their eyes. The creatures looked as if they were guarding the bridge, at least at one time.

"That's something isn't it?" Slash asked.

"It has obviously lasted for a very long time," Marky said.

As Levy looked off into the Wabasha Valley he noticed the Tower of Maytane.

"Look," he said to Marky and Slash.

Marky and Slash turned to see the Tower of Maytane standing off into the distance just as they had left it.

"Well, there is only one way for it to get closer," Levy said.

"The sooner we can get the stone, the sooner it will become safe," Marky said.

"Hopefully no more surprises with show up," Slash said.

The Wabasha Valley was just as difficult to cross as it had been before. Marky, Slash and Levy struggled to pull themselves through the marsh. Solid patches of land where spread out, still when they came to one, they took advantage of the break from the sucking ground.

A cool wind blew across the valley creating a slight chill for the three friends. The sky became cloudier and made dark patchy places through out the valley.

After some time of walking, they reached the back side of the tower. They walked up onto the solid dry ground which surrounded the tower and shook some to help relieve their legs of the muck around their paws.

"Well, we need to get around to the other side," Marky said.

"Hopefully Rago will give us the stone," Slash said.

Marky, Slash and Levy walked around the side of the tower. After turning from around the second corner, they saw Rago standing on the platform at the bottom of the crumbling old stairwell. They approached the stone creature and stood before him.

"No one shall past these stairs," Rago said.

"We have come for the first piece of the Stone of Afadavis," Levy said stepping forward. "May we have it?"

"There is no stone here for you, now go," Rago said.

"We know that the first piece of the stone is here," Marky said. "Gecko the Great has told us so."

"Gecko the Great would not just send anyone," Rago said without moving.

"It is us, the Chosen Ones," Slash said.

"It is the ones who sealed the Triangle of Holding?" Rago asked.

"Yes that is us, we have met before," Marky said.

"Why is it that you need this piece?" Rago asked.

"Someone might be after the Stone of Afadavis," Levy said. "We have to take the stone back to the Woods of Syrus and give it to Randor."

"Why would someone be after the stone?" Rago asked.

"We aren't sure but we feel that someone may try and take it from here forcefully," Slash said.

"Why?" Rago asked again.

"We think someone may want to activate the Doomsday Device," Marky said.

"That is impossible," Rago said. "The Doomsday Device was never to be used."

"We have to believe that it is very much wanted to be put into use," Levy said.

"By whom?" Rago asked.

"We aren't sure, but Randor has asked us to retrieve it so that it can be returned to him," Marky said.

Rago's head then slowly turned downward to Marky Slash and Levy. His eyes then lid bright red and then back to stone. His head then went back to its original position.

"It is you," Rago said.

"Yes," said Levy.

"Than you must be true in your desire to have the first piece to the Stone of Afadavis?" Rago questioned.

Rago then lifted his staff and uncovered a hole underneath.

"May you take it and be swift on your journey back," Rago said.

Marky, Slash and Levy walked up to the opening in the base under Rago's staff and looked inside. Marky reached inside and pulled out a larger version of the small stone. As he did the dust blew off of the stone revealing the markings on top.

"But how will we carry this?" asked Marky.

Rago then spoke the words 'Metephorus Ra.' This made the stone piece crumble to dust and blow onto the small stone and forge itself around it.

"Size will now be to your advantage," Rago said. "Repeat the words once you reach the Woods of Syrus and the stone will return. Now be off, for if the stone is in danger, then so are you."

"What can you tell us about the other pieces?" Levy asked.

"I have been solely responsible for this piece and no other; there is nothing I can tell you of any other piece," Rago replied.

"Very well," said Marky. "We will be on our way."

"Thank you," Levy said to Rago.

As Rago answered back he lowered his staff.

"May the pieces remain safe," he said.

"It will be safe in the Woods of Syrus," Levy said.

Marky, Slash and Levy then decided to head back for the Woods of Syrus as the Sky light began to disappear slowly.

"We can go until we cross the Aqua Bridge before the night light sets in," Levy said. "We can then set up for the night on the boundary and wait for the sky light to return to Randor."

"We should be able to reach that bridge in time," Marky said.

"But how will we find this bridge?" asked Slash.

"We must walk straight away from the tower and we are supposed to run into it," Levy said.

"Alright," Marky said.

The three began their journey toward the Aqua Bridge in hopes of crossing before the sky light ended. Walking back across the Wabasha Valley proved to be just as difficult, especially for Slash.

"Is it heavy?" Levy asked Slash.

"It is not heavy but I can tell a little difference in weight," Slash answered. "But I don't feel weighed down though."

"It is a good thing that Randor is going to deal with these two stones," Marky said. "I don't reckon we will be that lucky to have the next stones be powderized."

"Randor will have a solution regarding the other pieces, I am sure of that," Levy said. "Maybe they won't be much larger," he wondered.

Marky, momentarily became stuck in the marsh of the valley.

"This stuff is so difficult to walk through," he said.

"It wears you out faster than you would like to be," Slash said.

They continued to walk as the Sky light set further into the horizon. When they came to the Embarrass River they where forced to stop and search for the Aqua Bridge. They looked strongly in attempt to see the bridge but could not.

"I don't see the bridge anywhere," Slash said. "Maybe we are not close enough to it?" he wondered aloud.

"I don't remember Randor saying anything more than going straight away from the tower," Marky said.

"I think it is around here," Levy said. "But where not looking for the right bridge."

"But Randor said, the Aqua Bridge," Marky said. "Want more could that mean?"

"Well, he said it is called the Aqua Bridge," he said. "I don't think this is any bridge that we have ever crossed before."

Levy walked up to the bank of the river and stared into the shiny dark calm water. He stared at his reflection of himself for a moment.

"I think this bridge is made of water," he told Marky and Slash.

"Made of water?" Marky asked. "Are you sure?"

"It is just a guess," Levy said.

Then the water began to ripple gently and first, and then more vigorously. As the water stirred, Marky, Slash and Levy stepped away from the shore and watched with curiosity. The night sky created just enough light to light the waves created. Then the water began to rise out of itself and take the form of railings and a floor to walk on. When the activity stopped, Marky, Slash and Levy were staring at the Aqua Bridge.

The bridge arched gently over the wide river underneath. The floor of the bridge looked like a river in itself flowing over the Embarrass River. The water formed rails to keep anyone from falling from the bridge.

Marky, Slash and Levy were unsure about crossing the thin bridge.

"It sure does look thin," Slash said.

"You can see right through it," Marky said.

"It flows just like a river," Levy said.

"It must be safe to cross or Randor wouldn't have us take this way," Marky said.

"That's right; it has to be safer than Sikes Bridge," Slash said.

"This does seem to be quicker and safer than going back across Sikes Bridge that is for certain," Levy said. "We sure can't try and cross Sikes Bridge in the dark."

Levy walked up to the beginning of the bridge which had spilled over onto the bank. He touched the water bridge and was convinced that it was strong enough to hold their weight.

"I think this is alright," he said.

"Well there is only one way to find out," Marky said as he walked onto the bridge.

He walked far out onto the center of the bridge and hollered back.

"You won't believe this but it is rock solid," he said.

Slash stepped onto the bridge, followed by Levy. As they walked the water made bridge flowed around their feet like a small creek. This was a surprisingly refreshing feeling compared to the marsh of the Wabasha Valley. Once sure of the bridge, they hurried to catch up with their friend.

Once they reached Marky and the center, they noticed him staring at the floor of the bridge.

"What is it, is everything alright?" Slash asked.

"Look," Marky said.

Slash and Levy looked at the floor and noticed that they could see straight through the bridge in between the flowing ripples. Below they could see the Embarrass River flowing in the completely opposite direction.

"Wow," Slash quietly said to himself.

"Look at that," Levy said to himself.

After looking through the bridge, Marky, Slash and Levy walked the rest of the distance across the long bridge. Once on the other side, they were back in the Godway Region. However this time they were on the canyon floor instead of high above on the plateaus.

"It looks like we might get to be the first ones to cross the canyon floors," Marky said. "But not tonight."

"I am not sure if I see anything we can eat around here," Slash said looking around the ground as best he could in the dark.

"Perhaps the best thing to do is rest tonight and look for something to eat in the morning?" Levy wonder aloud.

"That sound like a smart plan," Marky said.

"I'm sure there is something around here to find in the sky light," Slash said.

Behind them the Aqua Bridge fell apart and with a large and loud splash, returned to the Embarrass River. This caught the attention of the three friends. They quickly settled down in from the shore a ways on the dirty ground on the edge of Godway Region. It would not be long before each one had begun to get tired and fall asleep. The last glimpse that Slash had was the night sky which consisted of other stars and twinkling lights. However his eyes too became heavy as he fell asleep.

Chapter 5

Return to Syrus

In the morning light Marky, Slash and Levy awoke to find a thick fog all around them. They could not see into the canyons of the Godway Region. This was the way they had to travel.

"I can't see anything," Slash said.

"Well we have to go this way," Marky said.

"Shouldn't we find some food first before we begin?" Slash asked.

"That sounds like a good idea," Levy said. "But let's stay within talking distance of each other alright."

"Right, we don't know what's out there," Marky said.

"I'll go this way if you want to go that way," Slash said.

As they divided up, the fog quickly covered their sight from each other. Marky used his nose to sniff the ground as he fought his way through the fog. Levy hugged close to the ground. The fog did fall to the ground; therefore Levy was able to just see under the blanket as he searched for food. Slash used his keen sight to see better through the fog than his friends. Soon Slash reached the bank of the Embarrass River and came across some bushes that bared a pear like fruit.

"I found something," Slash hollered.

"Alright, we'll meet you back the camp," Marky said.

Slash pulled several of the fruit off of the small bushes and drug them straight back in the direction which had come until he reached Marky, and Levy.

"What did you find?" Levy asked.

"I found these growing on some small bushes along the river bank," Slash said.

"Do you think it is edible?" Marky asked.

"Well, I think Randor would have said something if it weren't safe," Slash said.

Levy walked over to the fruit and took one in his mouth. He then walked back to his original spot and dropped his fruit.

"There is only one way to find out," he said.

Levy picked up the fruit and took a bit out of it and chewed carefully, then swallowed.

"My gosh, it tastes so good," Levy said. "It is kind of sweet."

Marky and Slash then quickly grabbed their own fruit and too ate generously. As they ate they could not believe how good the taste was.

"This is good," Slash said.

"It does taste quite wonderful," Marky said.

Soon they finished their food and were off into the fog of the Godway Region. The fog was so thick that they each stuck close to each other in order keep from becoming lost from one another.

"I can't see anything," Marky said.

"I think that if we can keep going straight we will reach the other side of the canyon," Levy said. "I remember when we were walking to Sikes Bridge that it seemed to be a straight walk back to the cliffs at the boundary line of the region."

"But how can we keep from going astray?" asked Marky.

"Maybe if we stay near the side wall of the canyon it will lead us to the other side," Levy answered.

"I sure hope that we don't find what has kept all the others who entered down here," Slash said.

"With this fog, I don't see how anything can find us," Marky said. "We can hardly see each other."

"Well, if there is something down in here with us, we need to be on the lookout," Levy noted.

Walking through the canyon proved to be quite easy considering that the fog made sight very limited.

"I can't tell if it is warm or cold in her," Slash said.

Levy began to think about what Slash had said.

"That's odd, I can't feel that either," he said. "I'm not warm or cold; I can't explain how it feels."

Marky reached up and touched the canyon wall and was shocked at what he felt.

"The canyon wall feels that way too," he said, "Maybe it is the fog," he added.

Deeper into the canyon they could hear the sound of small rocks falling down the side. The sounds echoed through the Godway Region.

"I hope thoughts are small rocks and they don't get any larger," Slash said.

"Surely we will have plenty of notice if they do," Marky said.

As they walked on the sounds became more consecutive and echoed louder. Levy paused and began to feel the ground.

"What is it?" Marky asked.

"Something is underneath us," Levy said.

"Underneath us?" Marky asked.

"Where being followed," Levy said.

Marky, Slash and Levy began to walk slowly again, and again the sounds followed them. They began to walk faster as the sounds became louder. Soon small rocks were falling in front of them as the walked.

"Stop," Levy said.

Marky and Slash stopped. Then from behind, a giant worm broke through the ground and began fall toward the three travelers. Marky, Slash and Levy jumped away just in time to avoid being hit.

The worm was black in color and made a howling sound as it raised back up into the air. As the worm rose back up, it released a large wave of heat followed by cold. This

Was enough to make Marky, Slash and Levy back away from the large worm. Without paying attention, they fell into a hole made by another worm and fell down about ten feet. They wasted no time hurrying to get out of the way of the worm.

The worm seemed to search for Marky, Slash and Levy and then gave up and returned to the ground. Soon the sliding rock sounds ceased. As they began to look at where they had landed they noticed a glowing lime green slime all around the worm made hole which was big enough for Marky, Slash and Levy to walk through.

"Maybe we should walk through hear to avoid being pounded again?" Marky said to Slash and Levy. "It looks to head straight in our direction."

"What if one of them things comes back through this hole again?" Slash asked.

"We should be able to hear it before it actually get to us," Levy said. "We can dig to the top no further down than we are."

"Walking through here it is then," Marky said.

After there close encounter above ground, they decided that walking through the hole would be the safest way to travel. The glowing slime created a perfect lighting source to see ahead. They walked through the wormhole trying hard not to rub up against the slime covered wall. Slime slowly ran down the side of the walls, as it did, the glowing lime green light glowed much brighter as it splattered the floor.

"What do you suppose that was?" Slash asked.

"Looked like a giant worm," Marky said.

"That thing must be the reason people have not been returning," Levy said.

"Well," Slash said. "At least we made it past one."

"One, yes," Levy said. "But we still have a far day's journey in hopes of reaching the other side."

"Let us hope that we do not come across anymore of them before then," Marky said while looking around. "I sure hope this will take us to the boundary with syrus."

Levy again looked ahead to notice that the wormhole in fact went straight ahead.

"We're in luck," he said. "It looks like it does go straight on ahead."

Marky, Slash and Levy walk for a short ways before Levy noticed something strange inside the wormhole.

"That's odd," he said was looking at the ceiling of the wormhole which was now dropping with water.

"What is it?" Marky asked.

"The ceiling of this wormhole, it's dripping with water," Levy replied.

Marky and Slash noticed the dripping water. The three friends looked down the worm made tunnel and noticed that the dripping water looked to be dripping more steadily further down.

"Where can that be coming from?" Slash asked.

"I remember seeing a river before when we were near Gecko the Greats lair," Levy said. "But we can't be anywhere near that far yet. Even if we ran, we couldn't make it that far that fast."

"Well something above us is wet, but we can't turn and go back we've gone a good ways so far to do that," Marky said.

"So what, just keep going?" Slash asked.

"We don't have much of a choice," Levy said. "We could go back but we have made it so far without seeing any of those worms."

Looking at the dripping water he continued, "Yes, I think we have to go ahead."

They continued onward carefully walking through the slime and dripping water. As they walked the dripping water in fact continued to drip faster and faster until the point came where the water slowly rained inside the wormhole. The water soon was up to their feet and slowly rising.

"We have to keep going," Marky said.

"The water is getting higher," Slash said.

"Maybe it slows down ahead, just as it began?" Levy wondered aloud.

Marky, Slash and Levy pressed on, wading through the water. Just as Levy had hoped, the water soon subsided again leaving the three travelers soak and wet. They each shook to relieve themselves of some of the water and continued walking.

"At least it was a good bath," Slash said.

"Accept for we're covered in that slime," Marky said.

"Look ahead," Levy said. "The tunnel turns."

For now the tunnel turned and headed in the opposite direction that they needed to go. Something would have to be done.

"You guys will have to dig," Slash said.

"Us guys?" Levy said smiling.

"There is no way I can dig as effectively as you two," Slash answered back. "You guys dig all the time. Besides I can't dig very well."

"I've never seen him dig before," Levy said to Marky.

"Trust me," Marky said. "He can't, he's telling the truth."

Marky and Levy turned to the bend in the tunnel and sized it up. They got side by side and began digging away with Slash pushing the loose soil into side opening. Then a strange noise caught their attention and made them stop. The tunnel whistled with the sound of pushing air.

"What was that?" Marky asked.

Slash walked away from Marky and Levy a ways to see what might be making the noise. As he looked the sound made a big splash and rushing air began to pass by. Slash could see the glowing tunnel losing its glow, something was covering the glowing lime green slime and was coming their way. Then it hit Slash what it must be, he took off back to Marky and Levy.

"The water is coming this way," he said.

The water?" Levy asked with a concerned look on his face.

Marky and Levy looked and saw the darkness gaining on them. They quickly turned and began digging fiercely into the wall, while Slash pushed hard to move the soil away. As he dug he kept looking at the approaching darkness. The water was in fact rushing toward them with great force.

"Hurry," Slash said.

Marky and Levy did not reply, they dug as fast as they could trying to reach the bottom of the canyon floor.

"Hurry," Slash said louder.

"We're there," Marky and Levy said at the same time as light shown through.

"It's here," Slash said running up to his friends.

Then the rushing water hit them and with a strong shove, launched Marky, Slash and Levy out of the hole like a cannon. Into the air they went until the water subsides and they fell to the ground.

They stood up and shook off again and looked around wearily. What they saw before them was something they could not believe.

"That's impossible," Slash said.

"I don't believe it," Marky said.

They were looking at the very cliff that they had walked along just a day ago. Off to the left they could barely see the glowing lights of Gecko the Greats lair. Somehow they had crossed the Godway Region.

"How did we cross that far so quickly?" Levy asked aloud.

Now before them was the high cliff leading up to the boundary with the Woods of Syrus. Marky, Slash and Levy stared up at the amazing feet before them in awe, but none the less, determined.

"I think we can make it if we take it slow," Marky said.

"The shapes of the rocks along the side look like they might make it pretty easy as long as we watch our steps," Levy said.

Marky then walked up to the cliff and began to start his climb when the ground began to shake.

"What is that?" Slash asked.

Just then another giant worm emerged through the ground. This worm was twice as large as the one they had encountered before. The worm made a high pitched moan and began to fall toward the ground. Marky quickly leaped onto the cliff as Slash and Levy leaped into separate direction to avoid the worm's crash. The worm crashed to the ground with such force that the floor of the canyon shook violently. Marky clung to the rock he was standing on for dear life.

Again the worm raised itself high into the air. Slash and Levy quickly got their feet and ran towards the cliff as Marky climbed higher up the side of the canyon. Slash reached the canyon wall first and quickly began to climb as the worm again began to crash to the ground. Levy did not have time to reach the wall and was forced again to leap to safety just in time to avoid being hit. This time the worm moved from side to side attempting find anything left on the canyon floor. Levy moved out of the way but found himself farther away from Marky and Slash.

"Try and go around," Marky said.

As Levy thought about heading around the worm, the worm drew back into the air and very quickly crashed back to the ground. Levy then took the opportunity to head straight for the cliff. Marky and Slash had continued moving up the wall and were now far out of reach of the worm and had stopped in concern for Levy.

Levy leaped to the wall and without hesitation moved quickly toward Marky and Slash. The worm slammed against the wall creating some small falling rocks to come down, still, Levy moved onward. Levy soon reached Marky and Slash as the worm moved from side to side attempting to detect someone on the floor. After several passes the worm stopped and withdrew itself into its hole and seemed to move on. Mark, Slash and Levy continued to climb the cliff wall. Painstakingly, they watched every step making sure that they kept good footing on the rocks. Although there was some room for climbing, there was little room for mistakes.

They became slightly nervous when they reached the halfway point. They now were very far up and had slowed the climb in effort to avoid mistakes.

"Watch this rock right here," Marky said. "It has a large crack in it."

Slash and Levy were each very careful in watching the cracked rock and stepping over it. As they climbed, the top of the cliff drew closer and closer until Marky was the first to grab the floor of the Woods of Syrus and pulled himself slowly over the side and to safety. Next Slash reached over the side of the cliff as Marky helped him away from the side. Levy then pulled himself up and reached the top. He then looked back over the side of the cliff and took a sigh after seeing just how far up they had to climb.

"That's a long way isn't it?" Slash asked.

"I still don't understand how we made it that far," Levy said while looking out over the Godway region.

"Well it means that we are closer to returning the stones to Randor and going from their," Slash said.

Marky walked over and sat down.

"At least we made it out of that situation," Marky said.

They three friends sat for a short time and looked out over the Godway Region in pride of knowing that they were the first ones to make it through the Godway Region and live to tell about it.

"Well," Levy said as he stood up.

"The sooner we leave the sooner we can return," Slash said.

Marky, Slash and Levy began into the Woods of Syrus in hopes of reaching the River of Guidence before the sky light ended. As they were entering the woods, Randor, Reamy and Kelso were entering the Wabasha Valley.

Reamy and Kelso found it easier to ride atop Randor rather than bare the crossing. For Randor it was easy to cross the marsh land and reach the Tower of Maytane. Randor moved quickly by taking large steps through the valley. It was not long before the three reached the Tower of Maytane. They came before Rago to ask about their friends.

"Who comes before the Tower of Maytane?" Rago asked from his platform.

"It is I Randor from the Woods of Syrus," Randor said.

"Why have you traveled so far?" Rago asked.

"We have come seeking our friends who are seeking the first piece to the Stone of Afadavis," Randor answered.

"You speak of the Chosen Ones?" Rago asked.

"Yes, have you seen them?" Reamy asked.

"I'm afraid they have already been here and gone," Rago asked.

"Did they retrieve the stone?" Randor asked.

"They do now have the stone in their possession and have since left," Rago said.

"How long ago have then gone?" Randor asked.

"They set out sometime ago, yesterday would put it right," Rago replied.

"Then they are deep into the Godway Region by now," Reamy said to Randor.

"Oh my, they are not safe," Kelso said.

"They went in the direction of the Aqua Bridge near the end of the sky light," Rago told the three before him.

"Then we know they will have remembered to go in my guided direction," Randor said to himself.

"To go after them would mean risking ourselves as well in the canyon," Reamy said with concern.

"We will have to travel back across Sikes Bridge and reach them before they return to the river," Randor said.

"The leader of the Mirrormites will be after them with two of the pieces," Kelso said with a worried look upon his face. "They are not safe."

"Then we must hope that our speed is more swift than their own," Randor said.

"If they are in danger, then may time be on your side," Rago said. "May you be off then."

Randor, Reamy and Kelso then quickly headed back in the direction of which they had just came. Hopefully, they would be successful in reaching Marky, Slash and Levy in the Woods of Syrus.

Sometime later deep with the Woods of Syrus, Marky, Slash and Levy were nearing the River of Guidence.

"We are almost there," Marky said.

"When we get there I think I'm going to eat some apples," Slash said. "My stomach is growling."

"At least when we return Randor will not what steps to take from here," Levy said. "That we can be sure of."

"It feels like these stones are pulling me toward the river," Slash said.

"Is it uncomfortable?" asked Marky.

"No it's not uncomfortable; it feels like a small nudge," Slash replied.

"Maybe you can be rid of the stones once we reach the river?" Levy said aloud.

"It's just over this hill," Marky said.

As they moved over the hill, they reached the river side. Marky sat down beside Randor's vacant desk; Slash walked near the wood line and grabbed an apple to eat, Levy water to the river and took a sip of its water then sat on the bank.

"I guess the Powder Troll was taken care of," Marky said. "I see no sign of him."

"I wonder where Randor is?" asked Slash with a full mouth.

"I'm not sure but he will surely show up soon," Levy said.

The sky light soon was gone and the night light shimmered on top the River of Guidence. Marky, Slash and Levy began to become worried about Randor not returning.

"What could have happen to Randor?" Slash asked.

"Maybe we should go and ask Reamy," Marky suggested.

Then one of the trees along the wood line opened its eyes and spoke.

"Reamy is not in the Creek Cave at this time my small friends," he said.

"How do you know this?" Levy asked the tree.

"I come earlier from my post guarding the entrance to the cave," the tree said.

"Do you know where either he or Randor have gone?" Slash asked.

"I'm sorry but I do not," the tree said.

"What if something has happen to them?" Marky asked.

"Maybe we should go and not stay here," Levy said.

"If something has happen then maybe the stones are in danger," Slash said.

"Then moving would be the best thing to do," Levy suggested. "If those stones are trying to lead us toward the next piece then maybe the best thing to do is go after it."

"We could walk until we get tired," Marky said. "At least we would be remaining in one place for to long."

"But what if Randor does return and finds us gone?" Slash asked.

Levy jumped up onto Randor's desk and stuck his paw into an ink well on the side of the desk. He then took his paw and made a print onto a piece of paper.

"There," Levy said as he jumped back down. "Randor will know that we were here."

"He would know then that we have gone on to seek the next piece of the stone."

"But can we cross the River?" Marky asked.

"The River of Guidence is very much crossable," said the tree. "Simply swim across."

"Thank you," Levy said to the tree.

The three walked to the waters edge and began to swim across the river. As soon as they began to swim, the river stopped flowing and allowed Marky, Slash and Levy to easily make their way across the river. Once they were on the other side of the river, it again, began to flow with gentle waves.

"I guess the first thing to do is walk to the other edge of the woods and then see what direction the stones are taking us," Marky said.

Slash and Levy shook themselves dry and waited for Marky to dry himself off.

This side of the river had few torches to illuminate the woods; Marky, Slash and Levy began their move into the second half of the woods hoping to keep moving for some time.

"I wonder where this will take us?" Slash asked looking at the combination of stones on his chest.

"Who knows," Levy said. "We haven't been this way yet."

"Maybe we will find good luck with this next stone?" Marky wondered aloud.

"I'm not sure," Levy said. "I think this one is going to be the hardest one to get."

"Why is that?" Marky asked.

"I don't know, just a feeling," Levy answered.

The three continued on through the night into the Woods of Syrus. As the night light moved closer to the horizon Marky, Slash and Levy became more and more tired. Still, they kept on, not wanting to stop just yet. They moved between the trees trying hard to stay awake and keep moving. Finally after some time they stopped inside a small clearing.

"Maybe we should stop here for a rest," Levy said. "We could use the rest."

"This does look like a good place to rest and eat for a while," Slash said.

Marky lay down and yawned, "This looks great, but we can't rest for to awful long, ok?"

"I think we will be alright," Levy said.

"It's getting a little chilly out isn't it?" Marky wondered.

"I'll take care of that," Slash said.

Slash raised his right paw into the air and flicked his wrist. Then a red mist appeared and began to swirl and sparkle. Then the mist quietly exploded, left behind was a small fire. Slash then lay down beside it.

"A nice fire to keep us warm," Slash said.

Then he remembered wanting food.

"Would you two like some food?" He asked.

"No," said Marky. "I think I am going get some shut eye."

"Ok," Slash said.

"I'm fine," Levy said. "I will eat after I wake up later."

"That's fine," Slash said. "I'm going to go and get some food from the trees, you two sleep well."

Marky laid his head to the ground and closed his eyes. Levy laid down on his side and took a long, slow, deep breath. Slash headed not to far into the trees to fetch his food and then get some sleep himself. He headed into the trees and began to look for fallen apples. He was only in a short ways when he found some at the base of a tree. He grabbed one and began to eat.

"This is good," he said.

"Thank you," said the tree above him.

Slash quickly swallowed his food and answered back.

"Who are you?" he asked.

"I am just another tree in this fair woods," said the tree. "If my visions are correct, then you are seeking the third piece of the Stone of Afadavis aren't you?

"Yes, but how did you know?" Slash asked.

"Sometimes I have visions that allow me to see things in the close future," said the tree. "I don't tell many about this ability so please keep it to yourself. I would hate to cause a scene."

"That's fine," said Slash. "Do you know why we are looking for the stone?"

"I know you are attempting to stop the stone from falling into evil hands, but that is about it for that reason," said the tree.

"But you do know that we are after the third piece," Slash said.

"Yes," the tree said. "I can also tell you that you shall be successful in finding the third piece."

"Where is it?" Slash asked.

"You are heading toward the Dark Valley inside Vitare Canyon," said the tree. "There is where you will find the third piece of the stone."

"My friend said he has a feeling that this piece will be the hardest to retrieve," Slash said with a concerned look on his face.

"The fox, yes," said the tree. "He has a gift of foresight but does not understand how to use it."

"His feelings are usually right," Slash said.

"On your journey you must trust in his feelings even if some may not be completely right," said the tree.

"Do you see something about our journey?" Slash asked.

The tree shook its branches gently and answered, "The Dark Valley is home to the Fire Starters. They are very isolated creatures and keep to their selves, however, when they are disrupted they can be very aggressive. You must quietly enter the canyon and retrieve the piece without disrupting their work process."

"Can you tell me anything else?" Slash asked.

"I'm sorry but I have told you all that I can foresee," said the tree. "Now eat and rest your strength. I must hibernate for the night myself."

"Thank you," said Slash. "Might I have your name before then?" he asked.

"I am Hayden," he said.

"It was nice to meet you," said Slash. "Mine is..."

"It has been my pleasure to meet you as well...Slash," said Hayden.

Hayden then closed his eyes and began to rest. Slash continued to eat before returning to his fire and lying down to rest. Marky and Levy were well asleep on the other end of the fire.

As fire burned on, with Marky, Slash and Levy all three asleep, an unforeseen creature entered the clearing and approached the three friends. The fire reflected only the shadow of the small figure. Marky, Slash and Levy were unaware of the approaching figure until the fire made a loud crackle and awoke the three. They then noticed what was creating the shadow.

"Nelty," Said Marky with a smile on his face.

Levy and Slash jumped to their feet and ran over to their old friend.

"Hello, their friends," Nelty said. "I was just telling myself, Nelty sure would like to see his friends."

"It sure is good to see you here," Marky said.

"It is wonderful to see you too," Nelty said.

"How did you wonder into the woods so early in the morning?" Slash asked.

"I had been wondering about my friends for some time and decided to come to the Woods of Syrus and see if you could be found," Nelty said.

"Well," Levy said. "We are very much found, why don't you join us around the fire while we get something to eat."

"I was just telling myself, Nelty it sure would be great to eat a small bit," Nelty said. "I would be happy to join you," he added.

So Marky, Levy and Nelty sat around the fire in the early light as Slash brought back some fresh apples and placed some by each of his friends. As they began to eat they did little talking so that they could enjoy the apples which never seemed to lose their taste. Nelty too enjoyed the meal quite well.

"So, where are you off to in this direction?" Nelty asked.

"We're heading toward the Dark Valley inside the Vitare Canyon," Slash answered. "I shouldn't have said that."

"What," asked Marky. "How do you know that?"

"I came across a tree last night after you two had gone to sleep that had the ability to se shortly into the future. He knew we were looking for the third piece of the stone and told me that the other stones would lead us into a place called the Dark Valley." Slash said. "Please don't say anything to anyone else, I promised I wouldn't but forgot all about it."

"You have our word that this trees secret is safe," Levy said comfortingly.

Nelty then shook slightly at the thought of the Dark Valley. He stood up and began to circle the fire.

"That is not good," Nelty said.

"Did the tree say anything else about where we are going?" Levy asked.

"No, only that some creatures lived deep in the valley called Fire Starters," Slash answered. "It said they were trouble."

"I have heard that before as well," Nelty said.

"What have you heard about these creatures?" Marky asked.

"They are a largely populated group that lives very deep into the Dark Valley" Nelty said. "I have heard that they are themselves made of fire. Very few have seen them in many hundreds of years. They live in the caves but it there is almost no light to see once you almost reach the valley. There is a mineral on the walls of the canyon that reflect the sky light and only allow a faint amount of light through."

"How is it that you know this?" Slash asked.

"Everyone has heard the telling of the Fire Starters and now you have," Nelty said. "One must be careful, I know where it is, it would be my pleasure to lead you to Vitare Canyon, and it isn't very far at all."

"If that is where we are going and you know how to get there, then please lead us if you wish to." Marky said. "Having another friend on the trip would be wonderful."

"I was just telling myself, Nelty, a longer trip would be good." Nelty said.

"It isn't far?" asked Levy.

"Not at all, in fact you almost camped near the boundary." Nelty said. "If you are ready now I can take you?"

"I don't see why we wouldn't be ready?" asked Marky.

"Let's get to that third piece," Slash said.

"We'll follow your lead Nelty," Levy said.

Nelty began his way through the trees, followed by Marky, Slash and Levy. As they walked Marky, Slash and Levy noticed that the landscape had gone from extremely hilly to surprisingly flat.

"You will be surprised at just how close you were to the boundary," Nelty said.

Before long they came through the other side of the Woods of Syrus.

"I give my friends the Vitare Canyon," Nelty said.

Now out before Marky, Slash and Levy was Vitare Canyon. A red soiled canyon that looked to be a giant gouge into the ground. The canyon stretched for many miles and looked to be not quite as deep as the Godway Region. Across the canyon on the other side, the ground was extremely flat and lifeless. Dust blew in swirls across the land with no particular place to go.

The four stared out across the canyon in simple awe over the change of terrain. Nelty pointed to their right down the canyon and motioned for them to begin that direction.

"In that direction, we shall find Keller Pass that is rumored to lead straight down into the Dark Valley," Nelty said.

"About how far is this pass?" asked Levy.

"You shall find Keller Pass will find you if you seek it out," said a large tree next to the boundary.

"You have seen it?" asked Marky.

"I see it once a day," said the tree. "The pass will come toward you; however you must make hast in reaching the bottom."

"Hast?" asked Slash.

"Keller Pass continuously moves itself along the canyon wall from one side to the other," The tree replied. "It will only stop for a brief moment in the sky light."

The tree looked up into the sky light and then looked surprised.

"Well it would appear that you four are in luck," It said.

"Luck?" asked Marky.

Then the ground gently shook, hardly noticeable, as the four looked around they could find nothing creating the movement. Then from the side of the canyon, protrusions began to immerge outward and linked together creating a gentle path being created down to the bottom.

"You must hurry, and not waste time," said the tree.

"Thank you," Levy said.

The four then quickly jumped onto the path and began their descent down the side of the fiery red canyon.

Chapter 6

Enter at Your Own Risk

Marky, Slash, Levy and Nelty ran down Keller Pass. Slash, being the fastest took the lead and was followed by Levy, Marky and Nelty. Since they had no idea of knowing how long they had before the pass drew itself back into the canyon, the four continued without stopping. As they reached halfway down the entrance began to shake and pull itself into the canyon wall.

"We have to hurry," Marky hollered.

As they ran further down the pass Nelty noticed that the pass was closing in on the four of them.

"I was just telling myself, Nelty, now would be a wonderful time to run faster," He said trying to stay up with Marky.

"Climb on," Marky said.

Nelty jumped onto Marky's back and grabbed the scruff of his neck tightly and rode with him. With Keller Pass closing in, Slash stopped once he had reached the floor of Vitare Canyon which overlooked the Dark Valley.

"Hurry, you're running out of time," he hollered.

Next came Levy who reached Slash as the pass closed on Marky and Nelty, who were still a short ways up. Marky ran as hard as he could but could feel the pass closing at his heels. At the moment that he felt the closing pass reach his feet, he made a great leap with Nelty on his back off of the pass and down to the canyon floor below. He turned around to find the pass return to the wall and disappear.

Now the pass that was suppose to take them down into the Dark Valley was gone. They now had to look out over the Dark Valley. The valley looked just as another canyon inside of a bigger canyon. Only the bottom could not be seen. Not too far down the light gave way to darkness and nothing could be seen beyond that.

"How are we going to get down into the Dark Valley?" asked Slash as he looked over the ledge.

Marky walked over to the side of the Dark Valley and too looked over the edge.

"We should be able to climb down the side of the valley as long as we move one after another," he said.

Levy and Nelty stared out across the Dark Valley in amazement of its difference from Vitare Canyon.

"Who wants to go first?" Marky asked.

"I will guide my friends down first," Nelty said.

Nelty then climbed over the side of the ledge and began his decent into the Dark Valley.

"Friends must be careful, it is a ways down," Nelty said.

Marky, Slash and Levy then followed. As they climbed down the ground crumbled below their feet. The light was still around but it was clear to the eyes that below the light would disappear and they would walking into almost complete darkness if not for some lucky strands of light that were about to get through.

"Do you think we will be able to find the third piece of the stone without being discovered by the Fire Starters?" Slash asked Levy.

"No," Levy said. "But we can try."

"I have heard that the Fire Starters are rumored to have poor hearing but keen sense of sight due to the darkness," Nelty said.

"Well, how are we to get down there?" asked Slash.

Just as Slash had finished his sentence, the ground below began to shake. A second set of stairs began to pull away from its wall and reveal itself. The stairwell went straight down into the heart of the Dark Valley.

"I was just telling myself, Nelty that does look like a great way into the Dark Valley," Nelty said.

Levy then took two steps to the beginning of the stairs. He stuck one paw onto the first step and watched his paw turn to black in the darkness.

With a deep breath Levy said, "Here we go."

Levy then began the walk down into the Dark Valley, followed by Marky, Nelty and Slash. As each one entered they quickly disappeared into the near lightless environment. As Slash began his walk down, he slowly watched as the world went from day to night within a blink of an eye. There was just enough light being allowed in that Marky, Slash, Levy and Nelty could just see each other and the stairs beneath them.

"I was just asking myself, Nelty, how far does this lead," Nelty said.

"I don't think we'll know until we reach the bottom," Marky said.

"Just be careful to watch the edge, it sure is awful hard to see," Marky said.

"So the Fire Starters, what do they look like?" Slash asked.

Nelty replied, "They are creatures of fire. Hundreds of flames joined together to create one unified soul. Other than that information I know nothing else," he said.

"So down at the bottom of this valley we are going to go up against fire, literally?" asked Marky.

"I am afraid yes," Nelty said.

"Why live way down here through?" asked Levy.

"All I understand is that they remain down here because of their grown sensitivity to the sky light," Nelty answered. "Those who have been here before say that the Fire Starters have their own lighting system powered by ore from the canyon walls. They mine this ore on a regular basis."

"It's good to know that we won't be in the dark once we reach the bottom," Slash said. "Except for being seen that sounds like a good thing."

The four walked onward for quite some time. Their eyes were adjusting to the darkness with every step.

However, back in the Woods of Syrus, Randor, Reamy and Kelso had returned from the Wabasha Valley.

"It would appear that our friends have not made it back yet?" Reamy asked.

Randor let down Reamy and Kelso and began to survey the area.

"Something doesn't seem right; it feels as though we have not missed them," he said. "They would not have strayed from the path that we have taken."

"But what could have happen to them?" asked Kelso.

"Do you think something has happen to them?" asked Reamy.

Randor then looked toward his desk and noticed the paw print that had been left behind by Levy.

"Oh, no," Randor said.

Reamy flew over to the desk with Kelso climbing up to the top to observe the paw print. This concerned them.

"What do you think of this?" Reamy asked Randor.

"I fear that it means that our friends have gone to seek the third piece of the stone," Randor replied. "They may be in danger."

"Should we go after them then?" asked Kelso.

"We could, but we have no idea of knowing in what direction they have gone off in," Randor answered. "With out an idea, there is no good chance to find them."

"Then what shall we do?" asked Reamy.

"I am afraid we have no choice but to wait and hope that they will be able to find the third piece and return safety," Randor replied.

"Then we wait?" Reamy asked.

"Yes," Randor said. "We wait."

As Randor, Reamy and Kelso prepared to wait for news, Marky, Slash, Levy and Nelty drew closer to the bottom of the Dark Valley.

"I see light down below," Levy said.

Marky looked over the side of the long staircase and too could see the light below.

"It sure is kind of an eerie red light, isn't it?" he asked.

As they neared the bottom they reached what could only be called piles of smashed rocks scattered all over. To the left and to the right were caves carved into the canyon. These caves seemed to be the source of the rock piles. The four walked up to the closest pile and hunkered down behind it.

"This must be what powers the lighting system," Levy said.

The lighting system was made up of old iron lamps placed all over the Dark Valley. Inside the lanterns was the rock inside burning with a dark red flame that made the environment the same color.

"I don't see anything around," Marky said.

"Perhaps they are in the caves mining," Levy said.

"I was just telling myself, Nelty it appears to be quite calm," Nelty said.

The surrounding was calm indeed. There was absolutely no wind moving to create any kind of breeze. There was only the light sound of an unknown object chipping away at rock inside the caves. As the four looked around more closely, they could see small ledges leading above the caves to what appeared to be smaller holes resembling built in houses.

"That must be were they live," Slash said.

"Then we need to watch not to disturb them," Marky said.

"But where to look?" Slash said.

"Maybe the stones on your chest will tell us," Levy said.

"I was just telling myself, Nelty, surely the stone must be in one of the caves," Nelty said looking toward the caves to the right.

"That's it," Marky said. "Let's walk slowly along the caves and maybe the stones will tell us again when we are close."

"They should lead us right to it," Slash said.

"Alright let's go find that third piece," Levy said.

Marky and Levy began to the next pile by hunkering down to the ground and slowly creeping forward. Followed behind was Slash and Nelty. The four moved from pile to pile while the force of the stones on Slash's chest grew stronger. Then from out of one of the neighboring caves came the sound of marching feet, growing louder with every step.

"Get down quick," Marky said.

The four quickly scattered towards two separate piles. Marky and Slash hid behind a small pile of rocks; peeking ever so slightly to see what was coming. Levy and Nelty ducked behind a small protrusion from the valley wall; they too carefully looked over the top of the rock to see what had been making the large sound.

As they each listened, the marching sound grew louder and louder. From one of the smaller caves to their right, the light inside grew brighter and brighter. Marky, Slash and Levy looked at each other as Nelty quietly shook as he watched the cave.

Then up from the cave came what had been making the noise. It was a troop of over fifty creatures that appeared to be that of walking flames. It was the Fire Starters, creatures made up entirely of small puffs of fire, with small legs and arms which helped carry a large canvas rug piled high with a fresh collection of the mined rocks. The Fire Starters pulled the rug over to an empty clearing across from the opening of the cave. After bringing the rug to a stop each one quickly jerked their part and from out from under the pile of rocks came the large rug and left behind was the pile. The Fire Starters then turned and headed back into the cave. As soon as they where gone, Marky and Slash hurriedly crossed the valley floor to rejoin Levy and Nelty.

"Did you see that?" asked Slash.

"They looked like walking fire," Marky said.

"I was just telling myself, Nelty, those were some of the Fire Starters," Nelty said in a very low voice.

"That was only some of them?" asked Slash.

Levy looked around at all of the dwellings built into the upper level of the valley walls and came to a quick assumption.

"Look at all of these homes above the caves, that could not have been all of them," he said.

"Remember," Nelty said. "Although they may be great in numbers they still do not hear so well."

"We should use that to our advantage then," Marky said. "The quicker we can find that piece of the stone and get back up to the top the better."

"Are we close to the third piece?" Levy asked Slash.

"It feels like we are close to it, but I won't know until we get closer for sure," Slash said as he looked down at the combined stones strapped to his chest.

"I would reckon that it would best to proceed before anymore of them come out of any of these other caves," Nelty said as he stared around at the Dark Valley.

Marky, Slash and Levy agreed and the four slowly crept out from behind the small protrusion in the wall. They carefully crossed in front of the cave which the Fire Starters had come out from and pressed onward. Moving from rock pile to rock pile, the four remained very cautious over their surroundings.

"We're getting closer," Slash said.

The four continued on a short ways before the stones caught Slash's attention.

"Wait," he said. "We passed it."

Slash then took a few steps back, and stopped. He turned in a circle and looked around at the sides of the valley.

"It's this way," Slash said staring toward the canyon wall to his right.

"But there's nothing here but the side of the valley," Marky said.

Slash paced back and forth for a moment before returning to the original spot.

"No," he said. "Its right here, it has to be."

Levy stepped back a ways to examine the canyon wall. He stared intently with a look of slight confusion on his face.

"But if this is the way to another piece, how are we to reach it?" He asked quietly.

Nelty shuffled up to the canyon wall and placed an ear against it and listened. After some moving around he stopped, his eyes got wider as if he had just become very intrigued.

"This wall is not as it were made to be seen," he said as he backed away.

Marky scurried up to the wall to have a listen. He raised his ear and pressed his head against the wall. After several attempts at moving he shook his head.

"I don't hear anything," he said. "Just nothing."

"I was just telling myself, 'Nelty that wall is hollow,'" Nelty said. "Perhaps what one is listening for, another's ear would never expect to hear?"

"But, how are we to get onto the other side?" Slash asked. "If we try and break through it, we might bring the Fire Starters back this way."

"I think it would be best if we all dig at the base, but hurry," Nelty answered after being shaken a bit by the sound of crackling rocks off in the distance that had begun. "I do not think this rock is as solid as one would think."

With that said Marky, Slash, Levy and Nelty united into a circle in from of the stone canyon wall and began to dig very feverishly but very stealthily. The four worked very quickly and paid close attention not to pile up onto another diggers site.

Then from out of one of the caves far down the canyon came a shimmering light which signaled the forthcoming of more Fire Starters. However the digging continued without hesitation. The sound of marching grew louder and louder until it could no longer be ignored. Slash looked up to see a small troop of 40 or so Fire Starters heading right for them. If it had not been for a small boulder beside them they would surely be seen.

"They're coming closer," Slash said as he looked back into the digging area, which by now, was becoming quite deep, so deep that the four could no longer be seen but the dust they were creating was visible.

Just then the sand in front of Levy began to give way, almost pour, into a small arched opening. Soon the opening was large enough to allow the four diggers access inside where ever it might lead.

Nelty quickly scurried inside, followed by Slash, then Levy, and closely behind was Marky. Once inside the four stopped silent as they listened to the marching group of Fire Starters pass right past where they were. Marky, Slash, Levy and Nelty listened to the marching grow more and more silent with every passing second. When it became near silence again the four took a deep sigh of relief and further paused to collect their thought and regroup their situation.

"That was far to close for my liking," Marky stated.

Levy looked to Nelty with wonder.

"How did you know this would be here?" He asked.

"I didn't," Nelty replied. "The wall sounded hollow by my ear and therefore I took the belief that a hollow wall could not run very deep otherwise it would sound much differently."

Marky began to look around but could not see much due to the darkness.

"I am afraid can't see much, it is too dark," He said.

Nelty then raised his right and began to make a swirling motion. As he did this, a pink mist began to appear and with a gentle flick of his wrist, he sent the mist bouncing forward. The mist hit the ground ahead and appeared to lose a small section of itself as it bounce further down the way. This small section became a small pink fire burning to light the way as did five other small fires that lit a straight crawl space for the four to follow.

"Doesn't seem to be too far of a ways," Slash said as he peeked forward.

"The third piece of the stone must be ahead," Levy said.

"I was just telling myself, 'Nelty had best let friends go first,'" Nelty said.

"What it wrong?" asked Levy.

"It is just that I am not sure what is at the end of this opening and I am sorry to be a bit frightened to lead," Nelty said ever so slightly trembling.

"Don't fear Nelty," Marky said as he walked ahead past him. "We will lead the way but stay close so that will be safe."

Nelty smiled and shook his head with approval.

Marky, Slash, Levy and Nelty followed the crawl space and just as Slash had proclaimed, the crawl space soon led into a dark opening that seemed to have no end. Marky first appeared out from the opening to find the small fire only lighting a small section of the ground past the opening. He walked to the edge of the light and tried his hardest to look around but to no avail. Levy then came through the opening and walked up beside Marky.

"Can you see anything?" He asked.

"Past what is lit, no," Marky replied. "It is complete darkness."

The two turned their heads to see Slash and Nelty crawl out of the opening and into the vast area of darkness.

"Wow," Slash said, "It feels like this darkness has no end."

"Why is that?" Marky asked.

"I'm not sure, I get the sense that this area is much larger than the one that we have just come out of," Slash answered.

Nelty then walked to the edge of the light and gazed out into the darkness with his eyes and listened very intently. He moved his head from one side to the other and slowly began to shake his head.

"You are right, the sound is much different," he said. "Very, Very far apart is the sound I am hearing."

"Sound?" Levy asked.

"Yes, the sound of openness," Nelty replied.

Nelty then walked over to Slash.

"Do you remember the method for fire I showed you on the Road to Tormor?" Nelty asked Slash.

"I think I remember but I am not sure," Slash answered.

Nelty then put his hands on Slash's back and side and coaxed him to the edge of the light.

"Just repeat after me and do as I do," Nelty said. "You'll do the work but I will show you."

Nelty then stuck out his hand forward into the darkness. Slash made the same motion.

"That's right way out there," Nelty said.

Nelty then again began to rotate his wrists, only this time without making the pink mist appear. Slash too did this as a hardly visible black mist circled his hand.

"That's it," Nelty said. "Keep on going with it."

As Slash continued, the black mist grew larger and larger.

"As you are larger than I am, you will be able to create a much larger fire burst than I will," Nelty stated.

As Slash continued the black mist had no almost smothered the light that was glowing from the opening behind Marky and Levy. Still he continued as Nelty instructed.

"Now when I say just give a gentle flick of the wrist and release," Nelty said as his face became no longer visible.

Marky and Levy watched with curiosity as soon they too were lost in the black mist. Then silence.

"Flick and Release," Nelty side from inside the darkness.

Slash then gave a flick and released the black mist which flew far ahead allowing the small light from the crawl space behind them to emerge again.

The black mist then began to glow far ahead. Soon it exploded into several smaller fires which flew to the side of the large cavern before the four travelers. As they fell into almost perfect distance from each other, each began to glow brighter. Soon it was a familiar but still strange site, black fires burning and creating light.

Now, with perfect light, Marky, Slash, Levy and Nelty could clearly see what was before them. They had crawled into a cavern so large that the four stood in awe. There would be no way that the ceiling could be reached even if all four stood on top of each other, that would not even get them close. The width too was quite impressive as well. If one were to run across from one side to the other, there would be no way to reach across without first stopping for a breath, even with the speed of Slash.

The Ceiling was held up by what looked to be six or seven stalactites and stalagmites connecting to make giant pillars reaching high over head. The water that had dripped for so many years had long since gone had left the pillars with a dry, dull appearance.

Then all four became focused on the center of the cavern. For there, wedged between an unconnected stalactite and stalagmite was the third piece of the Stone of Afadavis.

"There it is," Marky said with an intrigued look upon his face.

Slowly, Marky, Slash, Levy and Nelty walked across the floor of the large cavern. As they walked, the echoing sounds of steps seemed to chase each other as if in a race from top to bottom and from side to side.

"This place is huge," Slash said, which was followed by the echo of his statement.

"I've never been inside an area so large before," Levy said while looking at a pillar close by. He too was echoed.

"I was just telling myself, 'Nelty it sure was good to have those stones to lead us to this piece, we might never have found them here if it were not for them.'" Nelty said as he scurried across the floor with a rather pleased look upon his face.

"I've never been so privileged to hear so many different sounds bouncing from here to there," he added. "I so wish you could hear them."

"What do they sound like?" Levy asked.

"Much like quiet wind blowing in small areas, it is so wonderful though, with this much enclosed space the sounds have less time to escape my ears, and therefore I am able to make wonderful memories out of them," he replied.

As the four drew closer to the center of the cavern, the piece of stone they were searching for was growing more and more clearly visible. This piece was the largest so far that had been found. It was almost pie shaped but had a unique ring on the tip of it, giving the suggestion that it must be part of the side and center piece of the Stone of Afadavis.

"Quite strange looking," Nelty said.

"I don't believe I have ever seen anything like," Levy said.

Now Marky, Slash, Levy and Nelty were close enough that they stopped in wonder. The third piece was now before them.

"I wonder how we are to remove it," Marky asked aloud. "It looks solid?"

Nelty and Levy each walked up to the large formation to observe more closely.

"It looks to be wedged nicely but I'm sure it will come out," Levy said.

"What makes you so sure?" Marky asked as he and Slash too, approached the formation.

"Well, if it were me putting this here inside this location, I would not make it so hard of a place to find without knowing for sure only to turn around and make this piece impossible to retrieve," Levy said.

"Alright then how do we move than?" Marky asked.

The three friends turned to Nelty as if hoping he might have an idea.

"We could push it," Nelty answered as he shrugged his shoulders.

Levy sized the formation and the chuck of stone over to determine the best approach for the attempt. He walked around twice before stopping to one side of what appeared to be the backside of the stone.

"We should push from the side and maybe twist it out of place instead of pushing straight at it, that type of leverage should work," he said.

Marky walked around to where Levy was standing.

"It's a good shot anyways," he said.

Without hesitation, the two climbed the base of the formation and wedged a good footing into the ground and leaned into the stone. Slash and Nelty walked up before the pushing had begun but found little room left over for them.

Levy looked to Slash.

"Can you go in front and tell us if you notice any movement? he asked.

"Right," Slash answered.

Slash jumped down and began to run around to the front of the formation. Marky and Levy began to push themselves against the piece of stone. They pushed and continued pushing with all of their might. Slash reached the front of the formation and stood at the base to watch for any activity.

"Nothing yet," he replied.

Nelty then found a small opening and climbed up and too began to push with all of his abilities.

"I don't think it is going to move," Marky said.

The three continued to grunt and push. Soon the piece of stone began to crack and small dust particles fell from the connection with the formation.

"It's moving," Levy said with his shoulder firmly against the stone.

"You're right," Slash hollered. "It's moving."

As it crackled and popped, more and more dust fell to the floor. Soon the stone loosened, however, Marky, Levy and Nelty could not stop their combined force soon enough and the piece fell out of the formation and fell to the ground. With only one small flip in it, the stone fell at Slashes feet. It began to glow a brilliant gold color as it turn to dust and was absorbed by the concentrated orb that was around Slash's neck. This sudden absorption shocked Slash and made him take a step backward.

"Whoa," Slash said.

Marky, Levy and Nelty came down from the formation. As they did the echo of their footsteps bounced around the vast openness many times before escaping into the small crawlspace at the very far end.

"Are you alright?" Marky asked as he ran up to Slash.

"I'm fine," Slash replied. "It just startled me this is all."

Levy and Nelty quickly hurried up as well.

"I would reckon that you were lucky when that piece came out," Nelty said to Slash. "It almost hit you."

"Does it feel any more uncomfortable?" Levy asked.

"No, it feels…surprisingly fine," Slash replied.

Slash looked down at the responsibility that was around his neck as Levy turned to look at the fires burning all around.

"That's strange; I don't remember the fires making those crackling noises," Levy said as he looked around.

Slash hunkered close to the ground with a puzzled look upon his face.

"Do you feel that?" Slash asked.

Marky felt around but to no avail.

"What, I don't feel anything," he said.

"Wait a moment," Nelty said raising his hand and lowering it and walking away from the group just a small distance.

"What is it Nelty?" Levy asked.

"The sounds I hear are very different now," Nelty replied. "There bouncing everywhere."

Just then Levy looked to the walls of the massive cavern and watched streams of dust chase each other around across the walls.

"That's odd," he said. "It looks as though the walls are moving."

Then, from the high above in the peak of the cavern a small chuck of rock fell between Marky, Slash, Levy and Nelty. The four looked at the rock and then slowly up to each other as a faint crackling sound began to fill the air around them.

"Oh no," Marky and Levy whispered to each other at the same time.

Slash and Nelty knew what this meant.

"We've got to get out of here," Levy said.

"Hurry to the crawl space," Marky said as another small rock fell just beside him.

The four began to run across the wide stretching floor of the cavern towards the crawlspace from which they had first emerged from. As they were running a larger piece of the ceiling broke loose and came crashing down beside the formation that was home for so long to the piece of stone belonging to the Stone of Afadavis.

The crawl space from which they had once came from seemed so far away no matter how hard they each ran. Nelty, being the smallest had some trouble keeping up with Marky, Slash and Levy.

Levy had noticed that Nelty was trailing; he stopped as Nelty, who seemed to know why Levy had stopped, grabbed a hold of Levy's back and effortlessly climbed onto his back. Just then a section of ceiling smashed into the ground just a few feet from the two. Marky and Slash stopped.

"Levy, Nelty," Slash hollered.

"Hurry," said Marky.

"Come on," Slash said.

Levy quickly caught up with Marky and Slash and in the blink of an eye passed them. Just as fast, Marky and Slash race back up and the four made a mad sprint toward the crawl space. With the top of the cavern collapsing, Levy and Nelty reached the crawlspace first. Levy stopped at the opening and knelt down as Nelty slid off and scurried into the hole and disappeared. Levy quickly darted in and followed Nelty.

Marky and Slash reached the other side as pieces of the ceiling fell, putting out many of the fires burning. Darkness rushed towards them without hesitation.

"Hurry," Marky hollered.

"Ok," Slash shouted.

Slash went into the crawl space followed by Marky as the last fire went out. With the cavern collapsing, the four hurried along the crawl space for fear that it too would begin to fall in on them.

From far above the cavern, to the top of Vitare Canyon, a large section of the Canyon region fell in, forming a large crater. This crater could be seen very clearly from the edge of the Woods of Syrus.

As dust pushed its way out of the crawlspace Nelty came out from behind the large rock covering the opening. Levy soon pulled himself out and crawled far enough for Marky and Slash who were right behind.

As the dust settled, Marky, Slash, Levy and Nelty picked themselves up and incautiously wondered out into the open. The four stood looking at the side of the canyon wall, which had collapsed allowing a view clear across to the tri boundary of the Canyon Region with the Woods of Syrus and the Land of the Rock Gods. This view was lit slightly because it was so wide darkness could not completely shut out the light as it had inside the canyon.

"I was just telling myself," Nelty said. "Nelty, that is an amazing sight."

"Wow that has to be to or three times larger than the cavern was," Slash said.

"We were lucky to get out of there," Levy said.

Then Marky caught scent of something in the air. He raised his nose into the sky and took one sniff.

"Do you all smell that?" He asked.

The others raised their noses into the air but could smell nothing.

"No," Slash said.

"I am afraid I don't either," Nelty said.

"What is the smell?" Levy asked.

"It smells like...," Marky said taking another sniff. "Something burning."

The four travelers pondered for only a brief moment before realizing the same thing. They each slowly turned around to notice what over five hundred Fire Starters standing just off into the distance. Standing as a group, their burning exterior illuminated far up the canyon walls. Their eyes burned bright orange with a look of anger and disbelief at the intruders that had caused the noise that drew them out of the caves.

As they stood staring at each other, one Fire Starter stepped forward. Marky, Slash, Levy and Nelty stood in slight worry. Slash and Nelty each trembled gently as Marky and Levy stood unsure of the Fire Starters intentions. Then the Fire Starter shouted aloud.

"Trespassers," he hollered.

With that said, the entire mass of Fire Starters hollered and raced toward Marky, Slash, Levy and Nelty. Levy quickly looked back from the direction from which they had come.

"Hurry," he said. "Back to Keller Pass"

Marky, Slash, Levy and Nelty ran back toward Keller Pass with the legion of Fire Starters closing in on there heals. With pick axes in tow, the Fire Starters began swinging away hoping to catch the trespassers within their mists. Every swing drew closer and closer as Keller Pass came into sight. As the stairwell reemerged from hiding inside the canyon wall, Marky, Slash and Levy reach the base of the stairs with little time for celebration.

With one word Levy grabbed Nelty and threw him onto his back and raced up the stairs with due cause, following just as fast behind him, Marky and Slash gained one step after another sometimes missing a whole step if possible.

The stairway, being far narrower than the floor of Vitare Canyon, slowed the Fire Starters but did, in no way, derail their effort to capture those who they were after. As they filed onto the stairs what must have been the leader charged up at great stride as he and the others gained on Marky, Slash, Levy and Nelty.

"They're gaining on us," Slash said from looking behind him for a brief second.

"Look, up ahead," Nelty said to Levy pointing forward.

Levy was pushing hard for the daylight that was shining several steps ahead. As he had begun to tire from the steep strides he was making was hoping that Fire Starters would soon give up and discontinue their pursuit.

"Slash, look skylight," Marky hollered between deep breaths.

"Halfway," Slash said.

Levy emerged out of the darkness and into the sky light. This feat was that last thing on anyone's minds as Marky and Slash too ran right into the light without hesitation. As for the Fire Starters, the last step in the dark would be in fact their last step, fearing the sky light they stopped in the darkness as they watched the trespassers move further away.

"Hold, wait," Nelty shouted as he pointed behind them.

Marky, Slash and Levy stopped for the first time since beginning the climb up Keller Pass and turned to find the Fire Starters standing in the darkness and groveling and moaning in anger, shaking their pick axes and hammers.

"They won't come into the light," Marky said.

"Finally, a break," Slash said as he caught his breath.

"Let us not take to long getting out of here," Levy said.

"Out of here sounds good," Slash replied as he began to continue but in a slower pace as did the others.

Tired and distressed the climb to the top of Keller Pass would take time, however, sky light would still be shining once they reached the top. Levy, who no longer carried Nelty, reached the top and sat down at the edge of the Woods of Syrus. Next came Nelty, who was tired as well. Even though Nelty only had to walk half of the way up, that half was still a challenge for a creature of his stature.

Followed by Slash who was less tired but gladly took advantage of the cool shade next to the Woods of Syrus. Marky, who was last was most tired. He reached solid ground and instantly laid down.

With all four safely off, Keller Pass again withdrew itself into the confines of the canyon wall, disappearing until needed again.

"That was close enough for me this time," Slash said taking his last big breath.

"That was almost too close," Marky said as his breathing became less labored.

"We are the first; I believe to have returned from the Dark Valley," Nelty said. "I believe that this makes us very unique."

"I'll settle for very lucky," Marky said.

Levy caught Slash staring to his chest in wonder. He stood up and walked over with a cautious wonder.

"Which way are the stones pointing us towards now?" He asked.

"That way," Slash pointed.

The direction he pointed in was straight ahead.

"Oh dear," Nelty said. "That is towards Castlevania."

"That isn't much good I am afraid," Marky suggested. "There is no way to cross."

"To reach Castlevania you must follow the canyon until its end at the edge of the Land of Nothing, and then turn back into the direction of the pull," Nelty said.

"Then we will do that then," Levy said.

"Perhaps someone should return to the River of Guidence and inform Randor of our destination?" Marky questioned aloud.

Levy walked over to Nelty, who had been most helpful so far.

"Nelty, will you return to Randor and let him and Reamy no our whereabouts?" he asked. "We need that information to get back."

Nelty smiled and jumped up.

"I was just telling myself, 'Nelty that would be a wonderful idea,'" Nelty replied.

"Then will you leave know in hopes of reaching Randor my morning?" Levy asked.

"Most certainly I will," Nelty answered.

Nelty turned to Marky and Slash and acknowledged them.

"Until we meet again my friends," he said.

"You can count on it," Marky said with a smile.

"But be careful," Nelty warned. "Stay to the edge of the canyon while crossing the Land of Nothing, which is the home of the Terrance Hounds that roam aimlessly about. Be sure to stay along the canyon."

"We will," Levy said.

"Also, you will find food under the snows of Castlevania borrow in deep for shelter from the fierce winds and bitter night," Nelty added.

"Thank You," Levy said.

Nelty Smiled at his three friends.

"I shall now be off on my quest," Nelty said.

Nelty then turned and disappeared into the Woods of Syrus.

"Can we make it further?" Levy asked.

"A bit I reckon," Marky answered.

"I believe I can make it a ways before I want to rest," Slash replied.

"Then we're off to Castlevania," Levy said.

Chapter 7

Onward: Into Castlevania

As the Powder Trolls continued digging through the ground of The Land of Nothing, a Mirrormite returned to the Chiller who still could not be seen, as it was mounted atop of a Scrownge (Black Stallion).

"Sir," said the Mirrormite.

"Yes, Captain Crig, you have something to report?" said the Mysterious Chiller.

"Yes, Sir," replied Captain Crig. "Two of the Sky Crossers have returned with no report. One has yet to return."

Just as those words were spoken, the Sky Crosser who had battled Marky, Slash and Levy at Sikes bridge had been spotted in the sky. As it circled for a landing, its shadow cast over the digging Powder Trolls creating a quiet panic and fear.

As it landed in an area just down hill from Captain Crig, the Sky Crosser sat patently and awaited the captain's approach. Crig approached the dragon and quickly observed its torn wing before turning the blue night upon its back. Off from a distance it was clear to see that the captain was being brought fully aware of the situation that had happened. Then Captain Crig turned away and began his way back uphill toward the unseen Chiller. The Sky Crosser snapped the reigns of the dragon and the dragon began to walk over the hill side and out of sight.

"Sir," said Captain Crig.

"I trust that good news has been delivered Captain?" said the mysterious Chiller.

"Yes sir," replied the Captain. "The small piece of stone was discovered on Sikes Bridge. It has been identified."

"Identified?" questioned Captain Crig's unseen leader. "You mean you don't have it?" The Chiller asked with a strong tone. "Was the Powder Troll who escaped in possession of it?" it asked.

"No sir," replied Crig. "The piece was in the possession of a black creature not heard of before."

"This creature was very fast, much faster than those accompanying it."

"Others, who was with this creature?" asked the Chiller.

"Two other creatures never seen here before were by its side." answered Captain Crig.

"Really, and their descriptions?" asked the Chiller.

"They were four legged creatures," Captain Crig said. "The smallest with short fur coverings had the colorings of black, brown and white."

"And the other one?" asked the mysterious leader.

"The other was larger and was covered with long fur with the markings of red and white." said Crig. "They did appear to be on the journey together."

The mysterious leader, still out of clear sight, being blocked by a pink blossom tree, seemed to pause for a moment in thought before speaking again.

"Captain Crig, order your troops that we are packing up and heading toward the Wabasha Valley at once." said the unseen leader.

"The Wabasha Valley sir?" questioned Captain Crig.

"Yes, it is in the Wabasha Valley that I believe that we might find our three journeymen." answered the Chiller.

"Yes sir," answered Crig as he turned and headed into the encampment. "We leave at once for the Wabasha Valley at once, prepare for the journey," he said.

The army of Mirrormites began gathering their supplies and weapons. It would not be long before the entire army would be prepared and ready to march out of the Land of Nothing. As they began to march away, the powder trolls left digging stopped in confusion and wonder why the sudden withdraw. They all crawled out from their holes and trenches to see the Mirrormites marching off into the horizon.

Some time later, back inside the Woods of Syrus, Randor, Reamy and Kelso were finally returning from the Wabasha Valley. Worn out and thirsty, the three sat in order to catch wind and rest after such a long journey.

Reamy flew down to the ground besides Randor's desk as Kelso was slowly lowered to the ground by one of Randor's limbs. Randor himself rooted himself into the ground and began to relax.

"I don't understand," said Reamy. "There is no sign of them anywhere."

"Calm now," said Randor. "There is more than one path through the woods. Perhaps they have taken another road," he said reassuringly.

Kelso climbed from the ground onto the desk of Randor and sat down.

"I say," Kelso said. "I hope that nothing has happen to them."

"I have come to trust in their safety," Randor assured. "They have a unified power that has more than proven itself."

"Where have they come to us from?" Kelso asked.

"From a world not like our own," Randor replied.

"How is it that they came to be here?" Kelso questioned.

"They came to us from a connected gate that links our worlds together," Reamy stated while stretching his wings. "The gate has not been opened only but twice since its discovery."

"Why?" Asked Kelso.

"Only Hamel knows how to open and shut the gate," Randor said.

"Hamel, the master tree wizard, he still lives?" Kelso asked.

"Yes," Randor answered. "He guards the gate from their world, while the other side is guarded in our world by Reamy."

"But who is guarding it now?" Kelso asked yet again.

"I have closed the Creek Cave from the outside until my return so that I may be of service to Randor," Reamy replied.

Randor stood observing the woods around him when he spotted Kelso sitting on top of a piece of paper with a mark on it that he did not recognize. He leaned toward Kelso and reached for the paper underneath.

"Excuse me my little friend," he said.

Kelso stood up and moved to another part of the desk and sat again. Randor grasped the paper and brought it up to his eyes to read. He then took a deep breath and dropped the paper to the ground.

"I can't imagine," said Randor.

Reamy flew over and read the paper with the paw print on it as Kelso peeked over the side of the desk and too stared.

"Randor, what does this mean?" asked Reamy.

Randor paused, wide eyed, before acknowledging Reamy.

"This means our friends have already been here but have left," Randor replied. "I fear that they have gone in search of yet another piece of the stone."

"But will they not be in even more danger if they find another piece?" Kelso questioned aloud.

"Yes, I am afraid," Randor replied. "If they find the other pieces and are found by this stranger who is looking for them, then the worst might be set to occur."

"What should we do?" Reamy asked.

Randor uprooted himself and began to slowly pace. Kelso and Reamy stood in anticipation. Soon Randor stood still and looked at Kelso and Reamy.

"We will have to travel into the Desert Location and bring this matter before the Collective Council," Randor said. "I am afraid that this situation is far to grave to for us to do anything else. The council as a whole will be able to make a decision."

"When will we leave?" Reamy asked.

"We will wait until the skylight rise tomorrow," Randor said. "Until then we will rest from our journey, the night light will soon be here."

"I will return to Creek Cave and check on its safety and will see you at first break of the skylight," Reamy said.

Reamy then began to fly off toward Creek Cave.

"Very well," said Randor.

Randor then turned toward Kelso.

"You were very brave to have journeyed so far with the stone," he said. "As I told Reamy I had heard of you before and was certain that if I could make it into the Woods of Syrus and give you the piece then the stranger would not possess it."

"I was unsure what it was but I was sure that the Mirrormites had not the right to obtain it."

"It was a very wise decision that you made indeed," Randor said. "Now we will rest. You will find it quite comfortable on the desk next to the candle."

Randor moved one branch over a candle stick which was near the edge of the desk. The candle lit creating a soft and comfortable light. Randor then rooted himself into the ground and began to rest. Kelso moved closer to the candle light and curled up and began to rest in preparation for yet another long journey.

In another part of Mavenwood, Marky Slash and Levy had left the red, rocky climate of the Canyon Region and entered the jagged and ridged terrain of Castlevania. Castlevania was greatly clouded most of the time in the sky except for brief moments during the day when the skylight would shine through. Although the brightness would shine through, it would be for only a very brief time period before the light was again swallowed up by the dark clouds. Castlevania was extremely mountainous, however, the landscape was walk able thanks to wide section of the mountains sliced away to form very stretched out paths connecting mountain to mountain.

The horizon too was slowly leaving Marky, Slash and Levy behind. Tired and longing for a rest, they felt it was best to stop their journey for only the night and break.

"Perhaps it is best that we stop for the night and regain at first light?" suggested Slash. "It might be too difficult to carry on in the night light."

Levy stopped and surveyed the vast landscape of mountains and valleys and paths. He then looked to the sky which was becoming increasingly cloudy.

"I think it would be wise to stay," he said looking at a section of the mountainside arching outward, creating a canopy like roof over them. "This would make good shelter." he added.

"I could use the break myself," said Marky. "It's so cloudy here," he said gazing.

"If you two will begin a fire and create a place to warm around, I will go and see if there is anything in this new land to eat," Levy said.

"Food sounds wonderful," Slash said.

"It would be nice to end this day on a full stomach," Marky said as he walked under the overhanging mountain and began to push some small pebbles out of the way so that they would be able to lie down.

Levies took off carefully around the large overhang and climb above it and disappeared. Slash in the meantime, walked toward the clearing that Marky was preparing and gave a flick of his wrist and a swirl of dust began to twirl and explode into fire. Slash then comfortably set along side, as the weather was slightly cooler than it had been in the Canyon Region. Soon Marky was done clearing a bedding area around the fire and too began to have a slight chill.

"Quite cooler without the full skylight to warm us," he said.

"It is strange to adjust from not so long ago being hot near the canyon," Slash said.

Soon Marky nestled next to the fire and stared at what could have only been the setting horizon through the clouds as it grew darker.

It would be long before Levy come sliding back down the mountain side. The sound of the ground giving way beneath him broke the quiet sound of nothing but crackling black fire. Although it was becoming darker, Marky and Slash could see that Levy had something in his mouth.

Levy walked over towards his friends and dropped a large amount of vegetation with produce on the ends.

"I found these up the mountain a ways," Levy said.

Wide eyed Slash replies, "Potatoes?"

Marky walked over and examined the harvest.

"Looks like it," he said before sniffing. "Smells like it as well."

"There's only one way to find out," Slash said.

Marky stared to his side at the pebbles he had cleared away with an idea.

"Perhaps I can construct a structure so that we can cook them without burning them first?" he wondered aloud.

Marky began to gather the pebbles together with his nose and move them towards the fire. Soon he had a cone shaped structure with holes in the sides that was a perfect fit for the potatoes that Levy had found. The three friends each place three potatoes into their respective sides of the grill like structure. With the sizzling sound and warming smell of a meal cooking, Marky, Slash and Levy had begun to realize that they were extremely hungry. The instinct of hunger was easily forgettable inside the Dark Valley.

The black fire took absolutely no time at all warming the sincerely welcomed potatoes. Soon the tops began to split open. Quickly Marky, Slash and Levy knocked their meals out of the self made grill and onto the ground. They ate feverishly, for they had not a clue as to where the next meal would come from.

"Hey, these are potatoes," Slash said with a slight hit of joy.

"And darn good ones at that," Marky said with a full mouth.

As they ate the three travelers momentarily relaxed for ever so brief peace.

Unable to relax however, was Nelty. Nelty had made it deep into the Woods of Syrus in pursuit of Randor and company. For such a small creature, Nelty moved very stealth like and made barely a sound on the ground beneath him. As the night air was cool, Nelty's' hard breathing had created rings of mist as they left his nose. Although he was small in stature, Nelty had much built up endurance allowing him too few breaks on his trek. Even with speed and agility on in his favor, it was the hope of not only Nelty himself, but Marky, Slash and Levy's as well that Nelty reach Randor, Reamy and Kelso to deliver the news in time.

As Marky, Slash and Levy ate their meal atop the mountains of Castlevania, as Nelty ran with hast through the Woods of Syrus, and as Reamy rested inside the Creek Cave with Kelso asleep on the desk top along side Randor, the Mirrormite army was marching toward the boundary of the Land of Nothing with the Black Forest. Even such a large and massive army it was the Mirrormite soldiers, though mean as they came, were marching extremely cautious as they neared the Black Forest.

"My lord," Captain Crig said, marching up toward the mysterious Chiller.

"Yes captain, what is it?" he asked Captain Crig.

"Will our path take us through the Black Forest?" Crig asked.

"Yes it will Captain Crig," answered the mysterious Chiller. "Is there a problem with the path we are taking?" he asked.

"The soldiers are concerned, my lord," Crig answered.

"And why is that?" asked the yet unseen leader.

"This is the Black Forest, is it not where the Dark Shadow is said to reside?" Captain Crig asked with a rather calm and unshaken tone in his voice.

"Was captain, was," Said the chiller.

"Sir?" asked Captain Crig.

"Some time ago three strange creatures entered the Black Forest and was said to have battled with the Dark Shadow and defeated the spirit," the Chiller replied.

"How do you know of this Sir?" Captain Crig asked.

"I came across someone who gave me first hand accounts of the battle through his own eyes. Therefore I am not troubled by entering the Black Forest and you should see to it that your soldiers are not either." the Chiller said.

"Three never before seen creatures?" Captain Crig said quietly to himself.

The mysterious leader had heard this quiet question and replied.

"And it is the same three that I believe that the Sky Crossers saw at Sikes Bridge," he said to Captain Crig. "But why these three have returned, I have no knowledge."

After a brief moment of silence, Crig was ordered to fall back and disperse the news about the Dark Shadow. Crig fell back to the first row of marching troops; this row was of only eight lieutenants who then dispersed the news back through the legion of Mirrormites in time to enter the Black Forest.

As all of this was happening miles from Castlevania, Levy awoke during the middle of the night to the sound of a slightly chilly breeze blew through the valleys of Castlevania. He watched as the night light seemed to glisten and beam through the valleys. For a brief moment, Levy felt a sense of calm for the first time since their journey had begun. He laid there in the fire light and thought of home and how warm his bed would feel right then. But also, he could see how his world was protected by Marky, Slash and himself. This made him feel a sense of reassurance. Then he realized how cool the breeze was becoming and he drew himself back towards the dark fire and laid his head to return to sleep.

As the sky light began to rise slowly on the Woods of Syrus, Nelty raced, not knowing how close he was gaining to Randor and the others. As he ran, Reamy had come down from the Creek Cave just as Randor was stretching his branches and as Kelso was opening his eyes for the first time in the day.

"Randor," Reamy said as he perched on the desk next to Kelso.

"Aw, Reamy," Randor said. "I trust you had a good rest?" he asked.

"Yes, my rest was quite sufficient enough to last me some time," Reamy replied.

Randor turned to Kelso who was stretching on top the desk.

"You are looking much better now my friend Kelso," he said.

"Thank you Randor, I feel very well rested," Kelso answered back.

"When shall we be off Randor?" asked Reamy.

"Not very long from now indeed," Randor replied.

Just then from out from behind a large tree came a hard charging Nelty into the clearing. He quickly saw the three he was looking for and stopped just shy of hitting Randor's desk. With the sudden stop and the beginning of rest, Nelty quickly felt the aches of his hard pressed trek through syrus.

Nelty's arrival was a shock to Randor, Reamy and Kelso. They had not expected a Mort to be running through the Woods of Syrus.

As he sat for a moment gathering his breath, Randor noticed the red dust covering him from the Dark Valley. He quickly realized that this was not chance encounter and that Nelty had come to them for a purpose.

"My dear mort friend, you come to us from the Dark Valley?" Randor questioned.

Nelty had caught his breath and replied, "I was just telling myself, 'Nelty, I sure hope we reach Randor in time.'"

"You come searching for us?" Randor asked.

"I come bearing news from the Chosen Ones of days past," Nelty replied.

Randor's eyes widened as did Reamy's. Kelso crawled to the edge of the desk, curious to hear any news of the Chosen Ones.

"You bring news to us from the Dark Valley, yes?" asked Randor.

"The Dark Valley?" Reamy said shockingly aloud.

"Yes," Nelty answered Randor. "That is where we found another piece of the stone. That is where I have come from."

"They have acquired another piece and returned out of the Dark Valley?" Randor questioned to himself quietly.

"The Fire Starters, they still exist?" Reamy asked with intrigue.

"Oh, my," said Kelso. "I have heard terrible stories about them."

"I assure you that they very much exist," Nelty told Reamy. "I am also very sure that your stories are possibly true," he told Kelso.

"Nelty, is that your name?" asked Randor.

"Yes," Nelty said. "Please forgive me for not introducing myself."

"Please tell us of your news dear Nelty," Randor said.

"The Chosen Ones have obtained another piece of the stone that you seek and are being led by the stones into Castlevania," Nelty replied.

"Is there another piece of the Stone of Afadavis in Castlevania?" asked Kelso.

"I am afraid I am not sure," replied Nelty. "They began their journey in that direction but from the time that we separated until now I have no knowledge. Nelty said.

Reamy and Kelso looked to Randor with uncertainty.

"Should we follow them?" asked Reamy.

"If only we knew for sure in what location they were sure to be in," Randor said. "It is possible that they might be led into Castlevania for another section of the stone, but they might be crossing Castlevania into the Artic Region, and if that be the reality of things we will have no hope of finding them. Even more so if they cross into the Cold Climate Region," he added. "We will proceed with our original plan. We will travel to the Palace of Dry and inform the Collective Council of all that we know in hopes of aiding our three friends."

"And what can be done for Marky, Slash and Levy?" asked Reamy.

"I am afraid that they will be on their own," Randor said. "I can only hope that their journey will be a danger free one."

Randor paused briefly in thought, and then he turned towards Nelty.

"Will you accompany us on our journey into the Desert Location?" He asked.

"Travel with you to meet the collective council?" Nelty asked.

"Perhaps you will be able to describe the events which you, Marky, Slash and Levy saw down inside the Dark Valley," Randor said.

Nelty shook his head in agreement and stepped up to Randor.

"I was just telling myself, 'Nelty, it would be a wonderful honor to travel and meet the Collective Council,'" Nelty said.

"It is settled then," Randor said. "The four of us will leave immediately for the Palace of Dry and only hope that safety is on our friends' side."

Randor then reached a limb down towards Kelso. Kelso climbed from the desk onto the limb. As Randor raised the limb, Kelso made himself comfortable for the extremely long journey. With that, Randor stretched down a limb on his opposite side and extended it towards Nelty.

"This is a very, very long journey my new friend," he said. "You are welcome to ride among my limbs and a branch for as long is needed."

Nelty graciously climbed on. Randor raised his limb outward as Nelty attempted to make his surrounding as comfortable as possible as Reamy flew himself into Randor's canopy, and as the four turned to head towards the other side of Mavenwood, Randor's voice could be heard.

"Though our journey will be quite far and tiresome, it is my belief that we will arrive safely without much risk," he said.

As this journey was beginning, Marky, Slash and Levy were just awakening to their journey which was already in progress. Slash was the first to stand and stretch.

"How about another of those potatoes from diner?" he asked.

"I believe that would be a good idea before leaving," Marky said.

The three each threw another potato onto the homemade cone grill and dug in as soon as they were ready. After their morning breakfast was over. They each stretched with full stomachs while Slash kicked a mixture of pebbles and dirt into the dark fire, which toppled the homemade grill and extinguished the flame.

As the day progressed, Marky, Slash and Levy continued along observing the climate. The sky was completely clouded and the temperature had on risen slightly since the morning. Only every once in a while would the sun shine through, but that did little to create much warmth in Castlevania.

The path that was ahead of them was very smooth and very wide. Carved from the mountains to the side, this section of the journey was more relaxing. Off to the other side of the pathway was a 700 foot drop into the valley separating the parallel row of mountains. The day's breeze blew to simply remind Marky, Slash and Levy it was cool, not cold but rather a slightly frosted temperature.

Suddenly Levy stopped Marky and Slash from walking.

"Stop," Levy said putting his body in front of Marky and Slash.

Just in time too, for as Marky and Slash where looking across the valleys they had walked to the end of the pathway, at least for a short distance.

"Wow that was close," Marky said.

Slash crept up to the edge of the pathway and stretched his neck over the side. He could see that the pathway had collapsed and fell all the way into the bottom of the valley. Then he turned his head up the side of the mountains.

"Are we?" Slash asked Levy.

"I am afraid that it is the only way over this," Levy answered.

"Wooow," Marky said. "That is a good ways up."

"Here we go," Levy said, beginning the climb up and over.

Slash let out a deep breath as he began to climb as well. Marky began his climb, but not before looking down into valley.

The side of the mountain was not impossible to cross, it was rocky and jagged which made for good footing, but every step taken had to be felt out before applying pressure for fear of giving way and falling.

As they climbed the wind blew slightly stronger but surprisingly not all that much colder. The wind did however slow their progress over the hole in the pathway. They were forced to look to the side of the mountain instead of straight ahead. Talking was not possible because the wind seemed to steal every word like a thief in the night. Levy stopped for a moment and looked down to Marky and Slash. When he had their attention, he nodded his head up. Marky and Slash looked up to see a chuck out of the side of the mountain with a small platform that might just be large enough for the three friends to stop collect their bearings. Levy pressed onward and made it to the platform first. Levy realized that the platform was plenty big enough for the three of them and motioned for Marky and Slash. He also noticed the wind was blocked by a small part of the mountain which was not gone.

Next, Slash reached the platform and quickly pulled himself into temporary shelter from the wind.

"Wow, that wind is becoming fiercer the higher we climb," he said.

"I know," Levy replied. "We should be fine here for a moment."

Marky pulled himself into the safe haven squinting his eyes from the wind.

"I would never have thought that the strength of the wind would change so quickly, I am not sure if it would be wise to travel much higher." He said.

"I think we can travel straight across for another stretch and then we will have made it across where the path is out," Levy said. "Is that ok?" he asked Slash, who was in a fixation with something he was seeing across from the mountain.

"Slash," Marky asked as he walked over to see what was drawing his attention.

Marky looked over the wall of their safe haven and too was in awe of amazement.

"Wow, that's a sight," He said.

"What is it?" Levy asked.

"Come here and see," Slash suggested.

"Alright," Levy replied.

As he approached the small wall, Marky and Slash each turned their heads back towards the outside. Levy stepped up to the edge and looked out across Castlevania. He quickly drew a breath as he saw what was to be seen. Carved into a mountain side of a mountain two valleys away was a castle with large towers that reached outward into the sky, and a large stone carved wall reaching all the way around the front of it from out of the mountain itself. Although they had no idea what they were looking at, this was the Castle of Winge, the home of Zytor.

"Wow that is an awfully eerie looking castle," Levy said. "Is that where we have to go?" he asked looking towards Slash.

Slash looked down towards his chest where the collaboration of stones where joined. He closed his eyes and stood silent for a moment.

"No," he said. "We still have to move on in the same direction as before."

"I wonder what lives their?" Marky asked.

"Looks deserted," Levy said.

Just then a large gust of wind blew by their faces and the three friends ducked back inside for protection. The wind hit the side of the mountain and shot up towards the top, which stirred some harmless debris down towards Marky, Slash and Levy. They closed their eyes and covered their heads until the dust was carried away by the wind.

"We need to keep going," Levy said.

"How much farther will we have to go in this wind before we can begin back down towards the path?" Marky asked.

"It won't be that much farther, just a short ways is belief," Levy said.

"We are still heading in the right direction," Slash said. "So, I'm ready when you two are."

"Is that getting heavy?" Levy asked pointing towards Slash's chest.

"No, I will be alright through here," Slash answered.

With that said Marky, Slash and Levy stepped back out onto the side of the mountain and pressed on, away from the safe haven. The wind on this side of the mountain was not quite as gusty but did blow fierce enough that the three friends were forced to lower their heads again and continue carefully and blindly.

"We shouldn't be that far from the other side," Levy said turning whilehis back towards Marky and Slash. "We should start heading back down."

Heading back down meant that Marky, Slash and Levy could now see where they were going, but it also meant sliding down the mountain side little by little while still moving forward. Loose boulders and large rocks adorn the mountain side, which combined with the weight of Marky, Slash and Levy caused some larger rocks to give way but not before the three friends had passed on. As Marky, who was last, passed over a large boulder, it began to crack and pull away from the mountain and fall down toward the valley floor. Slash, who was second, quickly turned on top of, what he did not realize, was a very unsteady boulder as well. He stopped suddenly to see Marky paused right behind him, with a look of gratitude that he was not on top of the boulder when it gave way.

"That was close," Marky said to Slash.

Just as Marky had no more than finished that statement, the rock that Slash had stopped on, without warning, began to slide down into the valley. Slash had no time to jump, but rather was thrown off onto the mountain where he hurried to find a hold of anything that would keep him from sliding. The smaller rocks underneath him had begun to give way and he began to slide down as Marky and Levy both stretched out very far and grabbed him from each side.

This stopped Slash from falling into the valley, but Marky and Levy looked at each other with no real idea of how to lift Slash to a safe footing.

"I can't find a sure place to step anywhere," Slash said as he scurried to find one.

Levy looked up to a large rock protruding out from the mountain not far above Slash. He then looked to Marky and shook his head towards the rock. Marky looked up and then back towards Levy.

"Alright," he said to Levy.

"We're going to pull you up to that rock above your head, but you're going to have to be ready to grab a hold once we get you there because we might only have one shot at this," Levy hollered, into the wind to Slash.

"I'll be ready," Slash hollered back against the wind.

Levy looked to Marky and nodded his head. Marky nodded back as they took deep breaths and began to pull Slash slowly closer to what they all hoped was solid. Slash did his best to aid his friends by clawing his way up through the sliding pebbles and small rocks. Although the sliding rocks made it difficult for Slash but the effort he was making the effort by Marky and Slash more successful.

As the gritted their teeth and pulled Slash close to the rock above, Marky and Levy were beginning to lose their strength. Just as they could lift no higher Slash threw his right paw over the top of the rock and grabbed the front with his left one and pulled hard until he finally grabbed a good hold onto the rock and pulled himself onto it.

"I've got it," Slash hollered.

Slash pulled himself onto the rock and out of reach of Marky and Levy. Marky and Levy each quickly grabbed a hold of the mountain side so not to fall themselves. Once securely on the rock, Slash looked back over at his friends to check on their safety.

"Are you two alright?" asked Slash.

"I'm alright," Answered Levy.

"Fine," said Marky.

Slash carefully climbed down towards Levy. When he reached Levy he realized that Marky would not be able to continue, for he was still on the other side.

"You'll have to climb over," Slash said.

"Alright," Marky said.

Marky carefully dug himself into the mountain and began to slowly climb upward towards the rock that had just saved the life of Slash. As rocks and small pebbles gave way beneath him, Marky clung tightly to the mountain side. As he reached near the rock he slowly stretched out and took hold of the rock. With a large grunt, he pulled himself onto the rock to reach the halfway point.

"Be careful," Slash said. "I am not sure that this side is much more stable than the other. Just watch your footing."

Marky acknowledged but did not reply, for the wind was blowing strongly and he feared that he would not be heard. As he stepped off of the rock and headed down, a large group of pebbles gave way and Marky slid down the mountain side and right towards Slash and Levy. Wide eyed as he was closing on his friends, Marky took a deep breath, expecting and impact rather to be caught by Slash and Levy.

"Are you alright?" Levy asked as the dust cleared.

"Yes," Marky said. "I thought that I was going to knock us all over the side."

Marky took a deep breath in relief and smiled.

"We wouldn't let you go." Levy said as him and Slash smiled back.

Marky turned away from his friends to notice the landscape ahead of them.

"Wow, look at that," he said.

Slash and Levy turned to notice that the sharply peaked mountains of Castlevania were giving way to the snow covered and slightly sloped peaks of a new area.

"Looks like it will be a bit cooler?" Slash pondered aloud.

"Let's just hope that we are able to find another piece and move on," said Marky.

Marky, Slash and Levy carried on towards the snow covered mountains in wonder of Mavenwood's ability to simply up and change its scenery with little or no warning. As they left the missing pathway behind, they were hoping that the next piece to the Stone of Afadavis would not be too far into the cold before they could recover it and move on.

Chapter 8

The Terrance Hounds of the Artic Mountains

Heading through the Woods of Syrus, Randor, Reamy and Kelso began to discuss the Collective Council. Kelso knew very little of this subject but was most fascinated to learn. Randor and Reamy gladly educated his thirst for information.

"When was the Collective Council created Randor?" Kelso asked.

"The Collective Council was created more than four hundred years ago by respected leaders from all of the regions of Maven wood," Randor said. "The council was created to act as united body to resolve issues of safety and harmony within our world. Most regions of our world is represented with one seat on the. From the Artogs of the Artic Region to the not so pleasant Dark Guards of the Swamp of Great Loss, all are represented on the Collective Council."

"But how do the good and the evil coexist on the council?" asked Kelso.

"All of the representatives understand that we all must exist in order for Mavenwood to remain strong," Randor said.

"I am afraid I do not understand," Kelso said.

"Well," said Reamy. "Each of us does our part to maintain the splendor of Mavenwood, whether it is I taking care of Creek Cave or Randor overseeing the Woods of Syrus, our civilizations are all important to our overall survival."

"There is not always tranquility on the Collective Council," Randor said. "The Artogs tried to defend their kind by saying that he could be captured and shown the light, while the Scats of Hyden, who feared Zytor strongly, wished to see him vanquished. It is a balance of good and evil that sets our everyday world, when that balance attempts to shift, like now, with the safety of the Stone of Afadavis in jeopardy, that very collection of good and evil must set it right again."

"Please tell me more," Kelso said intriguingly.

"There are thirteen seats on the Collective Council," Randor said. "At the left hand of the table is Mayton who represents the Artogs of the Artic Region, he is followed next by Pulley who represents the newly formed Cold Climate region which is home to the scattered civilization of Chillers. Aside Pulley is Tapan of your people."

"Yes I know of Tapan, he is very caring but very goal driven," Kelso said.

"That he is," Randor replied.

"Now after Artimus is Hermit, king of the rock gods," Reamy said. "He is not the most pleasant to be around. Then comes Randor, then Gecko the Great from the Great Wall of Marketstan who leads the Collective Council.

"And the right hand of the council?" Kelso asked.

"Geron, a Tormite from Mortere Prairie, and Tram, the mort from the Canyon Region," Randor said.

"Hanger from the Desert Location is my favorite," Reamy said smiling.

Randor could not help but smile back.

"Hanger?" Kelso asked.

"He is leader of the Sundries of the Desert Location," Randor explained. "He is also oversees the Palace of the Collective Council. Next to him is the visionary, Latos, the elder scat from Hyden."

"Although Hermit is quite troublesome the next one on the council is the most devious of evil on the council," Randor said.

Reamy looked somewhat fearful of the mention of this council member.

"Who is that?" Kelso asked.

"King Salizon from the Swamp of Great Loss." Randor said.

Kelso raised his head in curiosity.

"Is that the person who once tried to over through Gecko the Great many years ago? I heard this story from long ago." Kelso said.

"It is the same that you have heard of," Randor said. "Only Hermit was behind King Salizon's attempt to head the council. Salizon was almost banished from the Collective Council but King Salizon is a very persuasive being and from time to time has surprised many by getting his way."

"Dare I ask who the last seat belongs to? Kelso asked.

"The last seat on the council has never been filled, for it belongs to a civilization that is believed to have been gone for some long years now." Randor said.

Kelso hung on every word that Randor was saying.

"It belongs to the Airwalkers," Reamy said.

"I have heard stories of them, and how they disappeared millions ago," Kelso said. "But why have a seat for someone who is no longer alive?"

"Out of honor for those who started life on our world," Randor said.

"See Kelso," Reamy said. "It reminds us of what we have and what we are given, and for that we are thankful. It is sort of a memorial," he added.

"However," Randor said. "The Council is not all that fill the Hall of Mavenwood"

"The Hall of Mavenwood?" Kelso asked.

"That's the wonderful cathedral room where the Collective Council meets."

"Oh, I see," Kelso asked.

"There are also the Knights of Zeste' Dore,'" Reamy said. "They stand guard in the four corners of the Hall of Mavenwood during all meeting of the Collective Council."

"Will I see these Knights of Zeste' Dore'?" asked Kelso.

"Yes," Randor said. "You may not realize this, but you have already met one."

"I have?" asked Kelso surprisingly. "Who?"

"Reamy," Randor replied. "He is one of the Knights of Zeste' Dore.'"

"Wow," Kelso said. "It is an honor to meet you, both of you."

"It is just as much an honor for us to meet you it returns," Randor said.

"What have I done to deserve such honor as the two of you have?" asked Kelso.

"You are the first to lay hands on the Stone of Afadavis in more than a million years," Randor answered. "When you found that small piece of the stone, you took it far from the evil that was searching for it and because of that very act of courage the forces of good have a chance of protecting the stone."

"It's that courage that creates the honor that we bestow upon you," Reamy said. "That is why it is just as much a pleasure of ours that we have met you," he added.

This statement brought a smile to Kelso's face, for he had never heard such a praise given to him before.

"I have never known the feeling of honor within myself before," Kelso said.

"It is with that honor that you go with us to the Desert Location so that the council will have the opportunity to meet the Powder Troll who has given us this chance we are given," Randor said.

"I shall make the most of my opportunity, thank you," Kelso said proudly.

"I believe you will do just that," Randor said. "You will also be fascinated to know that we are going to meet another Knight of Zeste' Dore' just ahead."

"Let us hope he is there?" Reamy said.

"Know just where to find him at this time of the season," Randor explained.

"I wish we knew what has become of our three friends that you speak of," Kelso said. "Do you believe that they are safe?" he questioned.

"I believe that they are...for now," Randor said cautiously.

Reamy began to look around with wonder.

"What has happen to Nelty? He asked.

Kelso began to look and found Nelty fast asleep in one of Randor's braches near his back. Nelty was nestled into comfortable position lying on his back snoring quietly away.

"There he is near the back," Kelso said pointing. "He is asleep."

"And a very well deserved sleep at that," Randor said.

Coming to the top of a gentle hill, Randor, Reamy and Kelso could now see out across the Land of the Rock Gods, with its rolling grass prairie and adorn with hundreds of large boulders whom inhabited the land.

"The Land of the Rock Gods," Reamy said as he was staring passed the Woods of Syrus.

Kelso peered up over the top of a branch that was in front of him to see the new landscape that was now before them.

"I remember this land," he said. "I came across this land many days ago although it was at night and I saw little of it around me," he added while looking around. "It is much more pleasing to the eye in the skylight."

Reamy looked though the vast landscape before flying down two branches closer to Randor.

"Do you know where he is?" asked Reamy.

"I believe at this time of the year we will most definitely find him at the top of that bluff," Randor replied.

Randor pointed to a small bluff not too far into the new land. The three walked into the grassy landscape and reached the bluff in little time.

Just as Randor had predicted, there was a large boulder at the top of the bluff. Randor reached the boulder and lowered his branch that Kelso was resting on.

"Now would be a good time to stretch yourself as we stop," he told Kelso.

Kelso jump off of the branch and stretched outward with a strength that he had not had since he had set out on his journey from the Land of Nothing.

Reamy flew into the air and reached his wings far and wide into the sky, flying high into the scattered clouds and then coming back down close to the ground, gently hovering between Kelso and Randor. Randor then reached his arm branch to the large boulder and touched it ever so gently.

"Awaken dear friend, it is your duty that we must now call upon," Randor said.

Randor then stood back. Kelso and Reamy to took heed and moved away. The large boulder began to move and grumble. Soon, two large arms reached outward and grasped the ground. The arms then pushed upward, lifting itself off of two massive legs underneath. Standing as tall as Randor, a neck stretched out a round stone head.

"Randor?" the boulder said as it turned around.

"Crete, Knight of Zeste' Dore,'" Randor said. "It is I Randor from the Woods of Syrus. I come with most urgent speed."

"A problem requiring the council's attention?" Crete asked.

"I am afraid that is just the reason for our appearance," Randor answered. "The council is gathering as we speak to discuss this grave circumstance we are facing?"

"Then as a Knight of Zeste' Dore,' I will make way immediately for the Hall of Mavenwood to stand post," Crete said.

"Please," Randor said stretching his arm branch to the shoulder of Crete. "Join us, as we are on our way there. I must inform my other constituents as to what we have learned in recent time."

"It would be my honor to accompany a member of the council to the palace," Crete said. "I am ready to leave at once," he added.

"Good, let us hope that time is on our side and that fortune is with us," Randor said while reaching down to pick up Kelso.

Kelso jumped back into Randor's branches and made himself comfortable. Reamy then flew high near the top of Randor's highest branch for a stronger view. All the while Nelty lay asleep, peacefully in the back.

"Let us hope that time is on our side," Randor repeated.

However, in the Black Forest the Mirrormite Army was proceeding onward. Even though the army was reassured by Captain Crig of the demise of the Dark Shadow, many of the normally fearless soldiers where cautiously and continuously peering about the trees on the chance that the story was untrue. The Black Forest was riddled with stone statues of those who had met the Dark Shadow and unfortunately lost their battles with the rumored spirit. Captain Crig, who was in front following the unseen leader, did not stray in the least bit from his duty. He carefully moved through the forest without touching a single tree.

"What my lord do we seek in the Wabasha Valley?" Crig asked.

"It's not what we seek but who," The unseen leader stated.

"Who, my lord?" asked Crig. "It did not know that the Wabasha Valley had any civilizations living within its borders."

"You are correct Captain," the Chiller said. "However there is one who guards the Tower of Maytane that I believe will hold our answers concerning these three travelers whom I believe are on the same journey as us."

"The Tower of Maytane," said Captain Crig with a sound of interest. "The home to the Dark Plague of Tormor?"

"It is my belief that the guard, Rago will submit information concerning are three enemies," the Chiller said.

"Rago is said to be very protective with information, are you sure that he will provide us with the needed knowledge?" Captain Crig asked.

"If he does not, we will bring him crumbling down," said the unseen leader. "Besides, I believe these three to be the very ones who entombed the Dark Plague of Tormor some time ago."

This statement intrigued Captain Crig greatly and with a look of determination he seemed to gain an increase in stamina.

"Then these foes will be worthy opponents for the Mirrormite Army," he said. "If three unknown creatures can defeat the Dark Plague of Tormor and destroy the Lord Zytor then my men will gratefully accept such a challenge."

"My Captain that alone is why I have asked for your services," the unseen Chiller said. "I am counting on it."

Just then, in the far back of the marching fleet a mirrormite soldier gently brushed aside a tree and started a chain reaction just the same as Marky, Slash and Levy had started when they where inside the Black Forest. The bark began to turn to dust and fall to the ground. As the dust cloud climbed the dark tree other mirrormite soldiers had stopped for fear it was the Dark Shadow. With growls and snarls, they readied for attack. Then half of the tree limbs turned to dust and blew away letting in a ray of light that beamed to the ground. The ruckus attracted the attention of Captain Crig, who turned around to observe the noise from his troops.

"You men stay with heading," he said. "The Dark Shadow no longer exists."

The troops snarled at the fact that this lone tree had shaken them. They quickly reformed there formation and took back to marching.

"Soon we will come into Mortere Prairie where we shall cross the Boundary River into Hyden from there we will follow the river to the Wabasha Valley," the Chiller said to Captain Crig. "I would not be surprised to find our enemies there as well."

"That would be a great reward at this journeys end," said Captain Crig as the Mirrormite Army continued marching towards Mortere Prairie.

As the evil army marched through the Black Forest, Marky, Slash and Levy had reached from the harsh winds of Castlevania and into a cold and ice covered mountain range which had slowed the three friends quite drastically. Through they were still on the same path that had began at the edge of the Canyon Region, the valley of Castlevania had given way to gentle sloping hollers that were more forgiving if Marky, Slash and Levy were to slip. The mountain tops, once rocky and dismally gray were now white with snow which blew around thanks to a more gentile wind.

The travelers had to dig their claws into the ice covered path. As Marky, Slash and Levy struggled to carry on, they had little idea that they were being watched. For off in the mountain tops, quickly moving, black, four legged creatures moved as if they were following the three and were slowly moving closer.

"It sure is colder than it was earlier," Slash said while shaking snow from his face.

"It's getting darker too," Marky said staring towards the fading skylight as it began to hide behind the mountain tops.

Levy then stopped in his tracks and stared behind him.

"What is it?" asked Slash.

Levy perked his ears to attention and tried to sniff the air, smelling nothing, he turned to Marky hoping that his strong sense of smell could tell him something.

"Marky, can you smell anything?" he asked.

Marky stuck his nose into the air and took two deep sniffs.

"No, the air is blowing the snow to hard for me to pick up any scent," he said. "Why, do you feel something?" he asked Levy.

Levy looked towards the mountain tops and carefully examined each mountain around him in one last hope of seeing through the snow.

"For a moment the wind blew over me and I had the impression that we were not alone here," Levy said. "Maybe it was nothing?" he questioned aloud with a glaring look on his face as he looked back to Marky and Slash.

"Maybe," Slash said. "But just to be safe, I am going with your feeling. We best find a safe place for us to rest for the night."

"Let's find shelter on the bend around this mountain," Marky said while pointing towards the path which was about to take a sharp curve around the side of the mountain and the wind seemed to blow very little.

"That sounds like a good idea, right Levy?" Slash asked.

Levy turned back towards the mountains which were covering much visibility with the blowing snowfall.

"Yes, that will be just right, up ahead," Levy replied.

Levy was the first to come around the bend of the mountain, saw the path make a sharp jig back away from them which made welcoming cove for him and his friends.

"There is a good place here for the night," he said to Slash and Marky.

Marky and Slash hurried around the corner, becoming tired and ready for rest. Slash quickly made for the side of the mountain and with no delay, created a black fire for warmth. Marky circled around a spot that he had chosen and laid down. After the fire, was in full formation Slash too, laid down for a spell. Levy however, stood at the edge of the bend with a look of uncertainty.

"What is it?" Marky asked as the fire made a shadow of half of his face as the skylight was fading completely behind the snowy mountains.

Levy turned and poked his head around the corner of the mountain and stared through the rows of mountains before him. He panned up and down with his eyes and slowly turned his neck back towards the path from which they had come.

"Nothing," he answered to Marky. "Nothing I guess."

He then pulled his head back from behind the mountain and turned towards his friends warming by the fire. Levy slowly walked over the black blaze and also laid down. He took a deep breath and slowly let it out.

Marky rotated his head as if he were stretching out. He shook his body with a surprised look on his face.

"What?" Slash asked.

"Now that we have stopped for a moment I should be completely exhausted but I only feel like taking a light nap," Marky said.

Slash did not immediately reply, he stretched his own neck and looked at the harness around his chest for signs of major discomfort.

"That's strange," Slash said.

"What's that?" asked Levy.

"I would think that this harness would be cutting into me after miles we have over come so far but it is kind of like Marky said, I only feel slightly ached," Slash replied.

Levy too realized that he was not as worn down as he should be. He figured in his head that his legs should be trembling from the distance walked from the rocky mountains to their current location, but, all his body was telling him was to break for a moment to reenergize.

"It has to be the Soul Dust from Gecko the Great," Levy said. "It is slowing the strain on our bodies." He then stretched his neck and said, "But I fear that it is wearing thin, we are starting to feel some reaction to the journey."

"Are we still on the right course for the next piece of the stone?" asked Marky.

Slash closed his eyes and felt the pull from the harness around his chest. He took a moment before he opened his eyes and replied.

"From the looks of it the path we are on is still heading in the precise direction, we are not off by very much if any at all," he told Marky, while looking ahead to the next bend in the pathway.

"Perhaps some rest will restore our full strength?" Marky said.

"I agree," Slash replied. "We don't know what lies ahead," he said to Levy.

"Alright then," Levy said.

Levy then laid his head down for a stint of sleep. Marky and Slash did just the same in hopes of a peaceful nap.

It was not long before Marky, Slash and Levy were asleep. The black fire crackled and popped, sending small sparks into the snow creating a small sizzle before burning out. The fire reached towards the night sky creating dancing shadows over the bodies of Marky, Slash and Levy. The three slept with out hearing a strange sound that was drawing closer. The sound was that of snow being packed off, into the darkness by the very four legged creatures that Levy thought that he had seen earlier. The sound drew closer and closer. The sound was coming down from the top of the mountain towards the cove lit by the fire. Then, just as the sound was about to enter the farthest reaches of the black fire it stopped.

Twelve sets of glowing silver eyes then appeared from the darkness and looked down towards the fire to see three Marky, Slash and Levy turned away from them with their backs to the mountain side. Then from out of the darkness the glowing green eyes turned into four black furred legs with white furred paws which led up a body like that of a very large dog covered with black fur and white spots. With long pointed, black ears tipped with white fur and a long black nose this creature with steel gray eyes was now completely visible. For it was the Terrance Hounds of the Artic Mountains.

Quietly growling the Terrance Hounds drew closer to Marky, Slash and Levy, a large spark crackled and landed near Levy. This slightly awoke Levy, who barely opened his eyes for a moment. As he close his eyes, Levy could now hear the stealth like breathing and quiet growling of approaching danger. His first instinct was to lay still only long enough to determine how great a danger he and his friends were in. He knew very quickly that there were several creatures coming down from the mountain for them. Levy turned his eyes towards the next bend in the pathway ahead of them and knew that Marky, Slash and himself would have to run. With a deep breath he jumped to his feet and hollered to his friends who had not even flinched in their sleep.

"Get up, run!" Levy yelled.

Marky and Slash quickly opened their eyes and without hesitation, jumped to their feet.

"What is it?" Marky asked.

"Behind you, run!" Levy yelled again while backing away from the fire.

Marky and Slash turned to see the twelve Terrance Hounds closing in on them growling. Although the Terrance Hounds had no teeth, their deep growl combined with their large size was truly freighting.

"Woo," Slash said with wide eyes.

Marky and Slash ran towards Levy who was moving towards the bend in the path. The Terrance Hounds each let out a large deep bark and leaped towards the black fire. Two of the Terrance Hounds effortlessly leaped over the flame and hit the ground which threw snow onto the dark fire putting it out.

The three friends raced around the bend onto a straight away leading into a long icy valley. Three of the Terrance Hounds jumped back onto the mountain side in pursuit, while three stayed on the path gaining on Marky, Slash and Levy. The three did not have to look behind them to tell they were being chased, they could hear the growling and stomping in the snow. Fortunately, the night sky light lit the icy path so that it could be seen through the blowing snow. It seemed that the Terrance Hounds had much better traction than Marky, Slash and Levy, which was true. The sharp claws of the Terrance Hounds dug deep into the ice allowing them to slowly gain on their targets. As the Terrance Hounds on the pathway gave great chase, the three hounds on the mountain side seemed to have a slight better advantage on the jagged ice of the mountain.

"Hurry," Levy said as he ran steadfast down the straightaway.

Even Slash, who was the fastest of the three, had difficulty running and carrying the responsibility of the Stone of Afadavis hindered him from breaking away at high speed. To their advantage though was a large boulder covering the path up ahead that might at least slow the three Terrance Hounds directly behind them down enough to get away. Marky, Slash and Levy each slid into the boulder and each other for that matter. The collision however, did not cause them to fall, rather, they each quickly separated from each other and began to scale the boulder. For Slash, the climb was much easier for him thanks to his arched claws. As for Marky and Levy, who had more straight and roughed away claws had to dig much harder to remain with Slash.

Slash reached the top of the boulder and quickly turned to see the danger behind him. As Marky and Levy were reaching the top, Slash could hear the sound of the Terrance Hounds closing in from the pathway and the mountainside. Then the sight of the glowing grey eyes nearing was enough to send a chill up his back. He shook the chilling feeling away in time for Marky and Levy to reach the top; they too turned to see their pursuers.

"Hurry, we have to get down," said Marky.

With reckless abandonment they each took a step down only to find the back side of the boulder twice as slick. It was impossible to cling to and the three friends slipped and rode the bolder to the icy pathway.

Lying on the pathway, Marky, Slash and Levy attempted to shake the cobwebs away before it they were seen. They looked at each other as if in agreement to stand up and continue running. Then from nowhere they heard a hollow voice call to them.

"Come inside, quickly, if you want to elude them," the voice said.

Marky, Slash and Levy stood up and rapidly looked around looking for the source of the voice who had spoken. Then Marky noticed a dark cavity between the boulder and the side of the mountain.

"Look, there," he said to Slash and Levy.

"Is that where it came from?" Slash asked.

Levy walked closer to the cavity in hopes of seeing what was inside, with Marky and Slash closely behind.

"Hurry, they are coming," the voice said.

Suddenly the sound of the Terrance Hounds was upon them, climbing the side of boulder. Marky, Slash and Levy each looked and each other and then back towards the voice. Levy shook his head up and down once to Marky who hurried towards the unknown voice and disappeared into the darkness.

"Go," Levy told Slash who went next.

Levy then ran towards the cavity in the boulder just in time to hear the Terrance Hounds reach the top. Only the path ahead could be seen through the darkness.

"Are they coming?" asked Slash.

"Please not a word," said the voice in the darkness. "They will hear you."

Marky, Slash and Levy stared towards the icy pathway as they watched the Terrance Hounds jump down from the boulder and continue on in there pursuit. They paid no attention to the dark cavity behind them as they ran on the pathway and out of sight. Marky, Slash and Levy did not move until they could no longer hear the barking.

"That was close," Slash said while still standing in the dark.

"Close, yes," said the mysterious voice. "But they will not travel to far a distance before they realize that they have missed you."

Marky realized that he was right next to the voice and turned in its direction, as he did he say a pair of glowing grey eyes staring straight ahead. He knew these eyes and ran out into the night light along with

Slash and Levy. They each turned towards the dark opening in wonder.

"Who are you?" Levy asked.

"Show yourself in the night light," Marky said.

"Very well," the voice said.

A very large Terrance Hound emerged from the darkness. With black and white fur stripes in the shapes of lightning bolts heading from the front of its body and ending at its rear. It to had black ears with white tips just as the others had, although this one was the largest of the ones chasing them, it moved very stealth like and made no sound.

"I am Nazereath, and this used to be my home land," the voice said.

"But your one of those things after us," Slash said.

"Terrence Hounds," Levy said to Slash.

"That is correct," said Nazereath. "How did you know, I've never seen any creature in Mavenwood that looks like the three of you."

"A friend of ours said to what out for you and your kind," Marky said. "He said you were dangerous."

"They are dangerous, I on the other hand am not," Nazereath said.

"I have to ask, why are you different? You certainly look more threatening than the ones that were chasing us?" Marky asked.

"Looks can be misleading my friend," Nazereath said slowly walking towards Marky, Slash and Levy.

Nazereath stopped short of the three travelers and sat down on the pathway.

"I used to be the head of the Terrance Hound pack," he said. "But I left when rampages across the mountains went beyond mere survival. I spend most of my time now inside the mountains and valleys of Castlevania. I saw you three from the moment you entered and followed you with curiosity and wonder as to who you were. It is a good thing that I did otherwise the pack chasing you might have gotten to you."

"Thank you very much," Levy said to Nazereath, while walking forward. "I believe that you may have been right."

"But you are not safe just yet," Nazereath said.

"What is that?" Marky said earnestly.

"You see once the Terrance hounds realize that they missed you at this boulder, they will turn back this way until they find you. Now why are you here and where are you heading to that could possibly be around here?" he asked.

"We are looking for something and we believe that it lies in this direction," Slash said pointing his head down the pathway.

Nazereath looked at Slash and noticed his harness with a glowing powdery yellow orb pointing in the direction of the Terrance Hounds. He stared for a moment,

and then stretched out his neck to sniff the orb. After sniffing his grey eyes looked away in wonder. He pulled his head away.

"The smell of this orb," Nazereath said.

"Yes," Slash said.

"I have scented this before," Nazereath explained. "And it is in that direction but you will meet the pack before you find what you are seeking."

"What do we do then?" Marky asked.

"You must ride the valley to the edge of the Artic Mountains and into the Artic Region. Only then will you slip past my old allies and head towards Artonia the only city within the artic region of any size. I was inside the city once and it was there that I caught that very same scent," Nazereath said.

"Excuse me," Slash said Nazereath, "Ride the valley?"

Nazereath walked to the side of the pathway and peered down into the slick and smooth valley between the mountains. He pointed his head down into the valley.

"Oh dear, sorry I asked," Slash said as he and his friends too peered into the valley below.

Marky noticed that the way down was not steep but it was quite smooth.

"How are we to get into the valley from here," he asked. "It is solid ice."

"You will have to glide off of the edge here and slide down into the valley," Nazereath said. "The valley floor is very slick, which will allow you to slide right past my old pack. Even if they were to see you, there is no possible way that they would be able to catch up. They will not bother you once you have entered the flat lands of the Artic Region. There you will be safe. A word to the wise though my friends," he added. "The Artogs within the city are skeptical of strangers but I believe when you tell them what you are in search of they will happily give you what you seek."

Nazereath again sniffed the orb around Slash's chest with interest.

"I must warn you that another is on the same journey as you three," he said. "You must be careful; I feel that this ones intention are not good."

"You can tell that from the scent?" Marky asked. "Amazing."

"A scent can give us Terrance Hounds the sense of foresight," Nazereath replied. "This orb is telling me that a missing piece of itself is in the hands of evil at this very moment, it is that evil which is searching for you as we speak."

Nazereath quickly looked up towards the pathway and then down to Marky, Slash and Levy with great sympathy.

"Now you must go, I fear that danger shall be coming back this way," he said. "Begin the climb down and slide to safety," he added.

"Thank you," Levy said as he walked away to the side of the path.

"Good Bye," Marky said as he did the same.

"Farewell," Slash said as he too did the same.

Levy began to climb down backwards into the icy valley, however it was not long before he slipped and began a rapid slide to the bottom.

"Wooooow," you could hear him say as he faded away.

Marky and Slash were not even as fortunate. They merely climbed over the side before sliding into the valley. They hollered as they too faded from Nazereath's sight. Just then the sound of the returning

Terrance Hounds came within hearing distance. Nazereath shook his head towards the new friends that he had made and turned around and returned to darkness between the boulder and the mountain side.

Marky, Slash and Levy slid quickly through the valley of the Artic Mountains. Levy spun himself around forward. He then looked far up the mountain side to notice the grey eyed Terrance Hounds returning back. As he stared, the dozen Terrance Hounds noticed him and his following friends. They quickly stopped and turned, they then began running towards Marky, Slash and Levy. However, from the pathway they would have little chance in catching them. Levy then watched behind himself as the hound like figures turned into glowing grey eyes and then disappeared all together. He then looked to see Slash and Marky farther back but having no problem gliding on top of the silky smooth ice sheet covering the valley floor.

Then Levy saw Marky and Slash looking passed him. He turned his head around to notice a large rock sticking out above the ice. He decided that it would be safer to jump onto it rather than attempt to slide around it. As he neared it he managed to stand long enough to make a giant leap onto the rock. He landed on the rock so quickly that he fell down and rolled over twice before stopping in time to avoid falling off of the other side.

Marky and Slash were coming up to the rock just as quickly and each attempted to follow that strategy that had landed Levy onto the rock. Slash however, slipped before reaching the rock and fell down. Marky leaped for the rock and just as Levy had done, fell down and rolled to the other side. Levy had just begun to help Marky to his feet when Slash hit the rock and rolled right up into him and Marky. They fell down again, but for the moment, they were stopped.

"Are you alright?" Levy asked Slash while standing back up.

Slash shook his head and replied, "Yes I'm fine but I was afraid I would have gone right over the top of you two and back down onto the ice."

"It was close," Marky said to Slash.

"We can't stay here though," Levy said looking down to the ice. "We passed the Terrance Hounds back up the valley and they turned after us again once they had spotted us. Although, they did not seem to want to enter the valley."

"Maybe it is far too slick even for them?" Slash pondered aloud.

"I agree though, we should not try our chances," Marky said.

The snow seemed to disappear into the ice as Levy peered onto the glacier around him. Marky and Slash stood and walked to the edge of the large rock and gazed ahead into the snowy white curtain that was barely see through.

"Are you two able to jump?" Levy asked.

"Ready," Marky said.

"I'm ready also," Slash said.

"One," Levy said.

The three friends stretched into a leaping position.

"Two," Levy said.

They each lowered their heads ready to jump onto the ice.

"Three," Levy said.

Marky, Slash and Levy jumped far, out into the air and landed on the ice and again began their rapid ride down the valley floor. Their warm bodies slide so fast down the valley that to speak to each other was nearly impossible.

Time would slowly pass before they could finally see the edge of the Artic Mountains and out into the white snow covered plains of the Artic Region. They could also see the valley floor was on collision course with a large mound of snow just ahead. There was no way to avoid the snow mound as it covered the edge of the valley floor like a boundary. Marky, Slash and Levy each hit the mound and flew into the air and out into the snow of the Artic Region. Snow flew wildly as they hit hard. When the snow ended the three friends laid unconscious, then a small shadow walked up and covered them.

"Look father," a voice said.

Another shadow, much larger appeared next to the smaller one.

"We must carry them home," another voice said.

Chapter 9

The Ice Palace of Artonia

Slash was the first to regain consciousness. He opened his eyes and saw himself staring up, not at the skylight but rather staring at a ceiling of rock and ice. He turned his head to see a small kitchen with an old wooden table and four wooden chairs around it. Directly across the table from him was a stone fireplace with a purple flame warming a large cooking kettle. As he watched the steam rise above the kettle, he noticed that the steam did not look hot but rather seemed to turned turn into a cold mist that disappeared into the walls around the fireplace. Slash quickly remembered Marky and Levy; he raised his head and began to look around the room. He found them, at the opposite side of the dwelling across from the fireplace were two small carved out niches were made into built in rock benches where Marky and Levy laid still asleep. Slash realized that he too was resting on the same type of bed.

Realizing that he and his friends were inside the home of someone he instantly reached to his chest and grasped the orb strapped to his body.

"We tried to free you from your harness to make you more comfortable," a voice said close to where the table was.

Slash turned his head to see the figure that had spoken to him. The figure was a big creature, not tall, big none the less. Standing upright and looking as if it were made of ice, Slash noticed the ice was merely a covering over clothing. With a bushy beard covered in ice and icy blue skin, Slash could not help but notice a similarity of this creature with someone else he had met but at the moment he could not remember. He laid his head back down to better clear the cobwebs.

"However we found that the harness would not come off by any means," the figure said. "Does it make you uncomfortable?"

"No," Slash said. "I have carried this for some time now and only feel the slightest discomfort possible."

"You are most fortunate that my son found you at the Artic Edge," said the creature. "We usually do not travel that far away from our home."

"The Artic Edge?" Slash asked.

"The boundary between our region and the Artic Mountains," the creature said.

"My son found you and your friends buried in the snow. You three must have taken quite a ride down the valley, hmmm?"

"Your son?" Slash asked.

"My son, Chill, he is the one who found your red and white friend first," he said.

Slash stretched and sat up, he did not say anything but was finally coming clear headed and well aware of where he was.

"Please forgive me, my name is Polar and my home welcomes you," said the figure.

Then, Marky and Levy began to stir. Levy opened his eyes first and noticed the purple fireplace. He raised his head and looked around to see were he was.

"It is alright," Slash said. "We are with friends."

Levy noticed Polar, who was sitting down at the table. Marky opened his eyes an immediately noticed the big ice creature and quickly sat up.

"What were are we?" Marky asked.

Slash jumped down from his rock bench and walked over to Marky and Levy.

"This is Polar, he and his son Chill found us at the end of the valley and brought us into their dwelling," Slash said.

"Please join us at the table we are about to eat," Polar said waving his hand across the wooden table covered with bowls and wooden spoons.

Marky, Slash and Levy each walked to the table and took a seat. Polar looked around the room for his son Chill.

"Son, you may bring in the course," Polar said.

A smaller version of Polar without the beard came from a hallway behind the table. He walked to the table and places a large bowl of blue snails and dark green lettuce. Chill carefully sat the bowl on the table and stopped to stare at the three creatures that he spotted in the snow.

"I've never seen anyone like you three before, where are you from?" asked Chill.

"Now son, do not question them as soon as they come to, that is not polite," Polar said. "Allow them time to gain their awareness first."

"Sorry father," Chill said backing away from the table. "Oh, father," Chill asked. "A chair for myself?"

Marky, Slash and Levy stood up and away from their chairs at the same time.

"Please have one of ours, we apologize," Levy said.

"Please be seated, no harm has been done," Polar said. He looked to Chill, "You may bring my chair from the den and sit upon it."

Chill smiled greatly and ran into the hallway and disappeared. Marky, Slash and Levy seated themselves and began to each pick out the dark green lettuce and place it in their bowls. Chill then came back with a wooden chair covered in Terrance Hound fur on the seat. He pushed the chair up to the table and hopped into eat and began using his spoon to dig out snails and lettuce. As he finished, Polar began to help himself to the meal. He placed the bowl back into the center of the table. Chill stood staring at Levy as he ate with out hesitation.

"You asked where we are from?" Levy said. "Well we are far away from you home, that is the only way I can explain it," he explained before eating.

"I've never heard of creatures like you three before in Mavenwood?" Chill questioned while biting into his snails.

"Well," Marky replied. "See that is because there are no creatures like us in Mavenwood. Our home lies beyond the Creek Cave," he said.

"You're from another world," Chill said wide eyed. "Father."

"Now, now son," Polar explained. "Friends none the less."

"Wow, it is a pleaser to meet you," Chill said.

"It is our pleasure to meet you as well," Marky said.

Chill sat in amazement of the orb around Slash's chest. He carefully watched as it glowed, inside were shapes of clouds moving around like if being blown by a breeze inside the orb. Slash noticed Chill staring. He looked at him with a smile.

"What is it?" asked Chill

"It is what we are looking for," Slash replied.

Chill took a large bit out of his lettuce not once taking his eyes off of Slash.

"Wow," he said. "How can you be looking for something that you already have?"

"Well," Marky said swallowing. "We are looking for pieces of it."

"Strange," Polar said. "It looks to be pretty well intact as it is."

"Should we show them?" Slash asked looking to Levy.

Levy looked at Polar and Chill, who had stopped eating and sat still with the look of pure intrigued on their faces.

"I think we can here, but only for a brief moment," Levy suggested.

"Ok," Slash said. "I think this is how it is done."

Slash stood up from his chair and walked to the center of the room. He stared down at the orb harness.

"Metamorphous Ra," he said.

The orb began to shine bright gold as a wind began to pick up inside the dwelling. The wind began to blow so hard that the spoons on the table began to blow off. Marky, Levy, Polar and Chill stood up from the table and walked towards Slash to observe this phenomenon. With the wind blowing in their faces, they watched as stone dust began to pure out of the orb and onto the floor. The dust began to swirl around on the wooden floor.

Three separate dust swirls emerged from the single circulation. As these three cyclones turned in unison, the sound of thunder began to rumble from wall to wall. The wind then died away and the three swirls of dust separately formed the three pieces collected along the dangerous journey. Once formed the pieces spun slower and slower until they stopped. Looking at the stones, Polar and Chill took deep breaths, Marky, Slash and Levy looked in puzzlement.

"Father," Chill said with a look and sound of fear.

"Oh my god," Polar said staring at the stones. He looked up at Marky, Slash and Levy and said, "Where did you come from, why are you here?" he asked.

"As we said, our home lies beyond the Creek Gate," Marky said.

"Yes," asked Polar in a stern but friendly tone.

"We set out from the Woods of Syrus on a journey to recover the lost pieces of this stone before something bad is to happen," Levy said.

Levy paused for a moment and stared at Polar and then at the stones.

"Have you seen these before?" He asked Polar.

"Not these exact pieces but a sibling to them none the less." Polar replied.

"You've seen the next piece we are looking for?" asked Marky.

"Well, not the stone itself but drawing of it," Polar said. "No one has laid eyes on the cursed stone since it was locked away a thousand years ago."

"The cursed stone?" Slash asked.

"Our ancestors believed that the stone was the source of the dark plague that ravaged our people two thousand years ago." Polar said.

"And for that it was locked away?" Marky asked.

"You must understand," Polar said as he sat back down in his seat. "There is no known way to destroy the stone, we have tried."

Slash looked down at the stones on the floor and said "Metamorpeus Ra." The stones then began to crush like light weight metal and collapse into there centers until there was nothing but dust which seemed to leap back into the orb again causing a glowing swirl inside. Then the glowing went away. Marky, Slash, Levy and Chill sat back down at the table.

"Will you take us to the stone?" Levy asked Polar.

"I fear that there may be no other alternative," Polar answered. "You three just might be able to rid us of this dreadful rock."

"Does that mean we will be going into Artonia father?" Chill asked

"I will be taking our three new friends into Artonia myself," Polar said. "I do not want you anywhere near that stone."

"You will wait here for the return of your mother and your younger sister."

Chill lowered his head and stepped down from the table and carried his bowl and spoon back into kitchen. "Yes father," he said.

"Now if you are finished eating, I feel that we should waste no time further without getting you to your destination." Polar explained.

Marky, Slash and Levy looked at each other a slight grimace of hope.

As a slim feeling of hope filled Marky Slash and Levy, the Mirrormite army had emerged from the Black Forest and was on the north road to Tormor heading south. The evil smug looks on the soldiers faces were in full view as they walked from the dimly lit forest and back into the bright skylight.

"See Captain Crig, as I had said, nothing to fear," said the mysterious leader. "Soon we will be with in the ruins of Tormor; there we will halt for the night and make our way for the Boundary River inside the Godway Region at first glimpse of light."

"Aye sir." Captain Crig said to his leader.

Crig stared ahead towards the horizon as the ruins of Tormor came into view as shadows of ruins buildings and homes.

"Sir, is it true what I have heard about a worf who inhabits the ruins of Tormor?" Crig asked. "I have been told that he is quite devious."

"Devious indeed Captain," said the unseen leader. "However he is the very informant I was talking about," he added.

"I do not trust this worf from the Dark Valley," Crig said. "Any Firestarter who changes into a worf can not be trusted."

"Now, now dear captain," said the leader, "I will do the worrying over this worf if his worth proves to be in question. Although with your army present we might not even come across his presence."

"It would suit me just fine if I did not have to come into contact with this creature." Captain Crig exclaimed. "Now sir if there are not further orders?" Crig asked.

"No captain that is the order until the first break of skylight," said the leader.

"Then I will fall back and inform the troops before we breech the lands of Tormor," Captain Crig said as he stopped, turned and began his march towards his troops who where a short distance behind him.

At the same time that Tormor was about to become the temporary home of the Mirrormite Army, Randor, Reamy, Kelso, Nelty and Crete had entered the Godway region. With the skylight fading into the horizon, Reamy took to the air.

"It will not be much longer before the horizon swallows the skylight," he shouted back down to his friends.

"Then I think it would be best if we took our nights rest atop of the plateaus. Randor wisely suggested.

"I agree," Crete said, "It would be a safe place, away from the Floor Worms."

"Excuse me," Kelso asked, "Floor Worms?"

"They are the creatures which burrow under the floor of the Godway Region," Crete said. "They could surface underneath our resting position and swallow us in on bite. If that were to happen, we would have no chance to notice it."

"I was just thinking that that would be a horrible fate," Nelty said.

"But do not worry," replied Crete. "The tops of the Plateaus are far beyond the reach of any Floor Worm. We will sleep safely tonight."

Reamy flew high to the top of a plateau just ahead and landed. Randor and Crete soon reached the base of the plateau.

"Now my two friends you must hang on as we climb to the top," Randor said to Kelso and Nelty. "To fall would be most terrible."

Randor grasped the plateau and stabbed his root in hard and began the climb to the top. As he began the climb Crete slammed his rock fingers into the rock of the plateau and pulled himself up. One off of the ground, he rammed his feet into the rock and pushed himself up further. The two giants climbed to the top of the plateau, Kelso and Nelty rested comfortably as possible with in the limbs of Randor's canopy.

"So, can you tell me anything of these three friends who are far away?" Kelso asked Nelty. "They seem so fascinating."

"The Chosen Ones defeated Zytor, some time ago," Nelty stated.

"Yes, I have heard that is what makes them so interesting to hear about," Kelso replied. "I would like to know about these friends that I have yet to meet."

"Well, I had the pleasure of first meeting them in the grasses of the Land of the Rock Gods," Nelty explained. "At first I was quite frightened of them, for I had never seen any creatures like them before; I have since learned that they are from a world that lies beyond the Creek Gate. I then led them down the road to Tormor; it was there that we met that unbelieving Worf, Grainger. He was a very mysterious creature, can and disappeared like the wind. We then left Tormor, however, the north road of Tormor led into the Black Forest and into the home of the Dark Shadow, who did exist then. I did not follow further; I returned to the Land of the Rock Gods, it was there some time later that I had learned of Zytor's defeat. I had not the opportunity to say goodbye to them before they left, therefore I was very pleased to find them outside of Vitare Canyon. From there, we began a new adventure as we ventured down Kellar Pass and into the Dark Valley."

"The Dark Valley, oh dear, oh dear," Kelso said with a look of nervousness.

Nelty did not boast or exaggerate his story; being humble he continued his story as openly and honestly as he could.

"Once we entered the Dark Valley and reached the bottom, we found the mines of the Firestarters," Nelty said.

"My goodness," said Randor. "Do they still exist?"

"Very much so," Nelty said. "It was down in the mines that the orb around Slash's chest pointed us to a secret underground cavern were we found a piece of stone that I learned was part of a greater danger."

"That you are right my dear friend Nelty," Randor said. "Danger indeed."

"As we left the secret cavern it collapsed," Nelty described. "This alerted the Firestarters and we were chased back up Kellar Pass out of the Dark Valley. Once we reached the top of Vitare Canyon, we part ways. I headed towards Randor with information and Marky, Slash and Levy headed towards Castlevania. Now I look forward the next chance that our paths cross," Nelty added.

"I too hope that our paths will cross," Kelso said.

Nelty looked behind himself and stared down to the ground.

"We sure are a long ways up already," he said.

Kelso turned around and noticed how far up they were and opened his eyes very widely in shock of the height.

"Is everything alright?" asked Nelty.

"Yes," Kelso replied. "I am simply afraid of heights, and that's a long way."

"Was just telling myself, 'Nelty, we are almost to the top though.'" Nelty said. "Once at the top we will be able to rest," he added trying to reassure Kelso.

Kelso turned and looked back ahead and noticed that they were gaining their way to the top of the plateau. Nelty also looked away and too was slightly glad not to be going much higher up.

"To be high up had not worried myself in the past," Nelty said. "But I am rather glad to be almost to the top."

Reamy backed away from the edge of the plateau as Randor stretched his limbs into the flat ground of the plateaus surface. Randor lowered his canopy to the ground, Nelty and Kelso jumped off and joined Reamy near the center. Then Randor dug his roots in deeply and pulled himself to the top.

"Ahhh, that feels good to reach the top," he said. "The rock is most terrible to root into, it is so hard," he added while stretching his limbs out.

Then out of the brief quiet, the pounding of rock on rock was drawing closer. Just when the sound reached the edge of the plateau it stopped, it was then briefly silent again. From over the side Crete threw his arms onto the surface and pulled himself into view and onto the top of the plateau.

"It is not so hard for me," Crete said. "I wish I did not have to be so hard on the rock to reach this place. To hurt the rock is not kind, but the rock will be fine."

"How far is our journey to the Hall of Mavenwood?" Kelso asked Reamy.

"We still have quite a journey to travel," Reamy answered. "Several days journey I am afraid to tell you."

"But fear not my little friend, we shall make it in due time," Randor assured.

"In the meantime, let us make some fire to light us as the skylight fades into the horizon," Crete said.

Crete then began to rub his hands together. The crackling and scarping sound of rubbing rocks cave way to smoke. Crete then placed his hands to the ground, the smoke then turned to fire as Crete removed his hands to expose a wonder orange fire burning not only to light the surface of the plateau but to also warm himself and his friends since being so high into the air meant it was considerably cooler and slightly windy.

"Randor," Reamy asked. "Does something trouble you?"

Randor did not reply, he merely stared off into the dark sky. The fire made his eyes appear empty due to the shadows but soon he turned to Reamy and acknowledged him. He briefly looked into the fire before turning to Reamy.

"I am sorry; did you ask something of me?" He asked.

"I was wondering if something was troubling you?" Reamy reinstated.

"I am hoping that Marky, Slash and Levy find their way through the mountains with out an encounter with the Terrance Hounds," Randor replied.

"I've seen them before. They would come to the edge of our lands on hunts," Kelso said.

"Did they hunt your kind?" Reamy asked.

"No," Kelso answered. "They did however cause quite a panic every time they approached our boundaries."

"I am quite sure they will be safe," Nelty reassured. "From being with them on journeys myself, I am positive that they will have the courage necessary to get passed anything that may come their way, even the dreaded Terrance Hounds."

Randor turned back to the fire for only a moment before looking back into the night sky in the direction that he hoped was favorable for his friends. He did not have know that Marky, Slash and Levy had indeed met the Terrance Hounds and had since moved on into the Artic Region were they were walking through the fresh snow with Polar as their guide.

As Polar led the way Marky, Slash and Levy each looked ahead and could see nothing. Though it was night time and not snowing, the night light clearly showed a large snow storm ahead that appeared to stretch on forever.

"Are we heading into the blizzard?" Marky asked from the end of the line.

Polar stopped short of the snowstorm and answered, "Yes, but it is not as it seems. We are heading into it and we aren't."

"I don't mean to sound puzzled, but how can we be and not be," Levy asked.

"You will see," Polar said.

Polar raised his right arm and placed it into the falling curtain of snow. He looked up high at the falling snow storm and began to hum. After thirty seconds he stopped.

"In the name of peace, open us to Artonia," Polar said before pulling his arm out of the snowstorm.

As he stepped back and joined Marky, Slash and Levy. They stood and watched as the curtain of snow began to open like a waterfall beginning to dry out. From the sky, the opening stretched to the ground in front of Polar, Marky, Slash and Levy. As the opening reached the ground, it quickly widened and allowed the four to see beyond it. What they saw fazed Polar in no way, Marky, Slash and Levy stood in shock and awe of the sight before them.

"This is Artonia," Polar said.

Polar stepped to the side as Marky, Slash and Levy stepped in line with him. They stood in wonder of the perfect cover made by the snowstorm curtain. They would have had no idea that such a sight would be hidden behind it. Before them were two large mountains that reached high into the air. The mountains were covered with ice which was lit like crystal by lights of homes and markets up and down each mountain. Torches by the doors and windows of these structures lit the ice to a level that there was not a dimly lit walkway in the city. Marky, Slash and Levy followed Polar into the valley between the two mountains. As they walked, they stared aimlessly up at the city of Artonia. The city seemed to reach into the clouds.

"We shall walk to the Great Hall," Polar said pointing to the left of the city.

"Is that were the piece of stone is located?" Marky asked.

"That is were it has been safely locked away from the skylight," Polar replied. "There, we shall meet with High Priest Frost; he will be the only Artog who can let us into the Ice Vault which contains the stone."

"Will there be any trouble retrieving this stone?" Levy asked.

"He will not likely open to the idea at first, but once you show him your stones just as you have shown me, I believe he will allow you to take this piece and rid us of it," Polar said as he guided Marky, Slash and Levy up the left mountain.

As they walked up the mountainside, Artogs young and old moved from house to house and building to building.

"It seems rather busy now," Slash said to Polar. "There is a lot of movement in this city, very busy."

"Dusk is always very busy in Artonia," Polar explained. "In a short time you shall find no one on these walkways, it will be emptied."

After some time walking Polar stopped in front of a large roman type structure with columns and giant stairs.

"We have reached the Great Hall," Polar said.

"Fascinating structure of ice," Levy said.

"Yes, we are quite proud of it," Polar said. "Now if you will excuse me, I will enter and inform High Priest Frost of your arrival."

"We will wait here for your return then," Levy said.

"Very well," Polar said. "I will not be long."

Polar walked up the large stairs and into the Great Hall. Marky Slash and Levy spent the time staring at the homes and buildings of Artonia. Artogs walked by and stared at the three strange creatures. Young Artogs were pulled away Marky, Slash and Levy as they tried to stop and stare.

"Seems quite strange to be seen as the odd creatures doesn't it?" Marky asked Levy, who paid more attention to the scenery than the oddity that they were creating.

"Slightly," he replied.

Slash noticed two small Artogs walking buy who did not look at them as though they were alien but rather with the look of acceptance, they smiled as they walked on by which prompted Slash to wave kindly.

"Some act as though they do not know of what is going on in the rest of the land," he said to Marky and Levy.

"Perhaps it is best not to worry the younger ones with knowledge of our journey," Marky replied while staring through the crowd and across to the other mountain with just as much traffic as his own.

"I wonder how far news of our journey has reached?" Slash wondered.

"I am afraid I am unable to answer your question," Polar said as he stepped back down the stairs. "But I can tell you that High Priest Frost will see you at once."

"We were hoping just that," Levy said.

"If you will follow me into the Great Hall," Polar asked

Marky, Slash and Levy followed Polar up the ice cold set of stairs and passed the long ice columns. Levy watched as steam like waves of ice blew from the columns in the wind. Marky stared at the floor and could see his reflection in it. Slash stared ahead as they entered the Great Hall.

The Great Hall had a wide open gathering room with solid ice floors and rock walls. The ceiling was a giant cathedral ceiling with very thin ice which was see thru like a window staring up at the mountain the hall was carved into. Corridors were carved into the rock walls on all sides of the Great Hall. The four walked to the center of the Hall and stopped.

"High Priest Frost is on his way," Polar said.

As they stood as sound was coming out of a side corridor. The sound was that of footsteps on the ice and it was coming towards them. Then out from the corridor walked a Artog wearing a red robe with a hood that were covered with ice. This figure was no bigger that Polar but seemed to draw much respect as Polar knelt to one knee before his presence. As the priest drew closer, Marky, Slash and Levy followed Polar's example and bowed their heads in respect.

"Please do not bow before me inside the Great Hall," the high priest said. "Inside it is not necessary. You may stand."

Polar stood, "High Priest Frost, these are the travelers I had told you about."

High Priest Frost stared at Marky, Slash and Levy with a half smile. Marky Slash and Levy noticed that he was and adult Artog that had no beard but rather a smooth ice blue face, noticing his smile, they smiled back.

"The Chosen Ones," the high priest said.

Marky, Slash and Levy looked at each other with confusion.

"You know us?" asked Marky.

"I take the time to know those who destroyed our dark lord," High Priest Frost said. "To me you are well known."

"Your dark lord?" Slash asked.

High Priest Frost raised his head, "Zytor," he said.

Marky, Slash and Levy stood in shock to learn that Artonia was the former home of Zytor. They looked at Polar and noticed the similarities.

"He did look similar to you but was dark black with red eyes," Marky said.

"Zytor was a wonderful scholar in Artonia, destine to take by place when my time ends in the future," High Priest Frost said. "Until he opened the Ice Vault and attempted to steal it."

Polar stood in shock of this news. "I knew nothing of this," he said.

"We believe the stone took control of him and turned him into the monster that you help defeat," High Priest Frost said. "And now I must ask why you have come for it?" He asked the three friends.

Polar turned to Marky, Slash and Levy, "Now you must show him as you showed me and mine," he said.

Slash shook his head in agreement, "Metamorpeus Ra," he said again.

Just as it had earlier inside the dwelling of Polar and Chill, the orb poured out onto the floor of ice and formed the three pieces of the Stone of Afadavis. High Priest Frost opened his eyes wide in shock and then formed a look of fear on his face. He looked around to be sure that no others had seen the three stone pieces.

"The cursed stones, quickly, you must put them away," he said.

"Metamorpeus Ra," Slash said again.

The stones disintegrated and reformed into the orb. High Priest Frost began to shake his head. Polar stood awaiting a decision from him.

"I think that at last, there is a way to rid our city of this cursed stone," High Priest Frost said to Polar. "Let us make hast, follow me."

The high priest led the four across the long room to a corridor that was not shining with ice but rather was dark thanks to the rock wall that did not reflect light inside. Once at the dark corridor, High priest stopped and reached into the darkness and pulled out a cone shaped torch that was not lit. High Priest Frost waved his hand over the torch.

"Igniteo," he said. This made the torch ignite.

The flame of the torched burned bright red. The light illuminated a set of stairs that seemed to curve downward.

"What you seek lies within the catacombs of the Great Hall," the priest said. "The spiral stairwell will take us down, but I forewarn you of this stairwell, at times the steps almost have you stepping straight. I suggest slow and cautious movement; fore these steps are very old."

"We understand," Levy answered.

"Fine, then if you will follow me please," High Priest Frost said.

Frost stepped into the corridor followed by Polar, Marky, Slash and Levy. The stairwell was not cramped but was narrow enough that to walk side by side was not possible. Levy had noticed that the walls of the corridor were not rock carved out of the mountain but were rather hand carved bricks placed together.

"You said that this stairwell is quite old, does that refer to this as being older than the Great Hall itself?" Levy asked High Priest Frost.

"Yes, the catacombs are the only remains structure left that remains from the Hall of Majesty," High Priest Frost explained. "When the hall was destroyed the Artog people cleared the ruins and constructed the Great Hall over the intact remains of the stairwell and catacombs were heading towards."

"My I asked what destroyed the Hall of Majesty?" Levy asked.

"Something that the three of you know all too well," High Priest Frost said.

He then stopped for a brief moment and stared back up to the three travelers behind him. Polar turned his head and looked at his new friends with a look of gratitude.

"The Dark Plague of Tormor destroyed the Hall of Majesty," High Priest Frost said. "Modock of Mortere Prairie destroyed what used to be a wonderful structure."

"But Modock stopped the Plague when he realized that he had lost control of it," Marky asked with worn looked upon his face.

"Yes, but the damage had already been done," Polar said.

High Priest Frost turned and continued down the steep stairs. Marky, Slash and Levy were extremely cautious with each step, for they were not built for creatures other that Artogs to walk down.

"When I learned that you three had sealed the plague back into its tomb, and that the Three Keys of Maytane had broken off inside the locks, I was pleased knowing that the plague would never again be set loose by magic or any other means," High Priest Frost said. "You three are wonderful heroes for our world."

Marky was following polar when he reached a step that was very short in width; he almost lost his footing but was able to keep his balance.

"Be very careful," he told Slash and Levy. "This step is very small."

Slash and Levy were both able to stretch themselves over the small step and on to the next one. Slash's foot gently rubbed against the small step which forced some pebbles to trickle to the bottom of the spiral stairwell. The pebbles trickled passed Marky, Polar and finally High Priest Frost before landing at the bottom of the staircase. As the pebble stopped, High Priest Frost stepped on it as he walked ahead.

As Levy finally stepped down away from the staircase, he could see nothing but his friends in front of him. He could see High Priest Frost at the front holding the red flamed torch, but past that however, he could see nothing but darkness. Slash then turned his head and gazed behind himself. He could see Levy fairly well but past him was complete darkness.

Slash turned his head back around in time to see High Priest Frost stop at was appeared to be a wall of ice.

"We have reached the Ice Vault," said High Priest Frost.

The priest then walked to the wall and reached his torch to a torch which hung on the wall. As the torch lit, High Priest Frost stepped back. The burning torch grew brighter and brighter, it the sparked a torch straight above it to light. This torch burned brightly as it lit one more torch above it. This torch lit two torches to the side of itself which in turned lit two more torches straight down. These seven burning red torches then showed the resting place of the so called cursed stone, the Ice Vault. The Ice vault was very large, Marky, Slash and Levy could have stood on top of each other and not been able to reach the top of the vault door. Made of pure ice so thick that it was not possible to view through it. In the center of the vault door was a round handle with six bars protruding from the circle handle. To the left side were two giant rock pin hinges which held the vault door into place. To the right side was a long lever sticking out from solid rock. The lever was made of ice which glistened slightly from the burning flames.

High Priest Frost walked to the center of the door and stood.

"Polar, will you bring be me the pull rod," he asked.

Polar shook his head and reached for a long staff which hung from a mantle beside him. He grasped the staff and brought it into the light. It had a three fingered claw chiseled on the end of it. Marky noticed that the staff was made out of a material like nothing else around him. Marky pondered quietly to himself as Polar took the staff to High Priest Frost. Polar placed the staff into the priest's hands. High Priest Frost noticed the curious look upon Marky's face.

"You are puzzled, why, I may ask?" asked the priest.

Marky replied, "Your staff, it spears made of something not from here?"

"You are quite right," the priest replied as he placed the staff's claw on one of the six bars in the center. "This is forged from rock gathered in the Hills of Gainstorm. Over the years we have decided that if the vault were to ever be opened again that the dial would be so hard. They would require a pull rod stronger than any material we possess here. The rock from Gainstorm is the strongest in all of Mavenwood."

High Priest Frost then grunted softly as he pulled down on the staff, forcing a quarter turn on the circular handle. He then removed the staff and backed away.

"Polar, if you would kindly pull the lever," he asked.

Polar pulled down on the lever of ice, as he finished, a loud thud echoed inside the catacombs. Silence emerged again if only for a brief second.

"Wow," Slash said after feeling the force of the thud.

The silence was broken by the sound of creaking hinges and falling ice particles so fine that they looked like dust. As the sound grew, the vault door began to open.

"We must stand way back," Polar said to his friends.

As everyone stood far back from the vault, the large door swung open showing nothing but a large dark void inside. High Priest Frost took his torch inside and lit a torch to his right. This torch, just as it had outside the door, began to ignite other torches one after another until they lit up a gigantic square vault with rock walls covered with a sheet of clear sparkling ice. The red torches also illuminated a thick round pedestal which sat in the center of the vault. High Priest Frost moved in followed by Polar, Marky, Slash and then Levy. They walked towards the pedestal and stood around it. On the pedestal was a large section of the Stone of Afadaivs.

"Friends I give you the stone that we have so feared," High Priest Frost said.

Marky, Slash and Levy banded together to gaze upon the stone. The stone looked quite out of place inside its surroundings which gave off an eerie feeling that reminded the three travelers how grave their journey was. Levy then noticed that there where three lines grooved into this piece.

"What do the three lines mean?" he asked High Priest Frost.

"Scholars have said that it is phrase for which your dark friends spoke up inside the Great Hall." He then walked over to Slash. "When you spoke those words, and I saw with my own eyes what you had brought to our forefront, it became my solemn belief that you will be able to rid us of this dreadful rock."

"To rid us of this, would bring a great peace to our city," Polar explained.

Marky, Slash and Levy, who had begun to look more worn and dirtied, stared back at the stone and the marking left upon it.

"Are you ready for one more," Levy asked Slash.

"I'm ready," he replied.

"May you take it and go," High Priest Frost said.

Slash walked onto the pedestal, as he did, his orb began to glow as did the stone before him. It began to turn to ash and swirl like a cyclone right into the orb. As it did Slash knelt in brief pain from it.

"Are you alright?" Marky asked.

"Yes," Slash said standing back up. "That was just a much larger piece that is all."

The orb stopped glowing and Slash returned to his friends.

"Alright to leave?" Levy asked Slash.

"Yes, of you two are ready," He replied.

"I'm ready," Marky said.

"Then let you three be on your way, I will escort you outside the Great Hall," High Priest Frost said. "Polar, will you kindly lead the way."

Polar led the way back up the spiral staircase and outside of the Great Hall. It had been a must faster trek up the stairs than it had been going down. As they stood out side, the once bustling walkways of Artonia were now empty and silent. Marky, Slash and Levy stared around in fascination off how in just a small amount of time such a busy place could become so scared. All that could be hear was a gentle little wind that was blowing by with reckless abandonment.

"So quiet for a once busy city," Marky said.

"Is there to be no one out at this time?" Slash asked.

"Artogs are family oriented; they see no need to be out after the coming of the night light," High Priest Frost explained. "From time to time you will see someone out on the walkways but that is only on rare occasion," he added.

High Priest Frost noticed a beguiled look upon Levy's face as he looked around.

"Why do you have such a look upon your face?" He asked Levy.

"This place," Levy said. "It seems to be so untouched, so innocent compared to any other place that we have seen."

"We are quite fortunate to be able to keep live the same steady pace, despite what is happening in the rest of our world," Polar said.

"Well, we should be leaving," Marky said.

"Before you leave, let be give you some information that will help you on your next leg of journey," High Priest Frost said stepping to the edge of the walkway which seemed to have a splendid view of the city. "Many years ago, a Chiller from the Cold Climate Region entered Artonia with a smaller piece of the stone looking to trade for it. We immediately had him removed from the city."

"Removed?" Levy asked.

"Oh peacefully of course," the priest replied. "We explained why we would not trade with him, it was a very pleasant denial, the Chiller has since been into our city without the stone on very friendly terms." High Priest Frost took a deep breath, "His name was Zim and I believe that to this very day he in fact still possess that piece of stone. Return out from the city and travel past Polar's home straight on until the rising of the skylight."

High Priest Frost then pointed in the direction. Marky and Levy both looked to Slash, who knew if that was the direction that the orb was pulling him in.

"Is that the right direction?" Marky asked.

Slash closed his eyes and felt the direction the orb was pulling.

"Yes that is in the exact direction," he answered. "Almost straight passed from which we had come."

"I will wish you a most successful journey and bid you on your way, High Priest Frost said. "Please return without the stone any time you will though."

"Thank You, we will," Levy replied. "Thank you," he added.

"Believe me when you return in the future and the news of your taking of the stone, it will be most welcome," High Priest Frost said. "Polar will see you as far as his dwelling outside of the city but then you must stay straight on until you reach Zim's."

The priest then turned to Polar and placed his right hand upon Polar's left shoulder with pride.

"Thank you for bringing them to me," he said to Polar.

"No thanks shall be needed your grace," Polar said. "Friends, we should be on our way now, so that you can find your stone."

Marky, Slash and Levy bowed their heads to High Priest Frost as he did the same for them. They then followed Polar back down the walkway and finally out of Artonia.

Chapter 10

Betrayal in Tormor

As darkness rolled in over the remains of Tormor, the Mirrormite Army built small fires through out the city and had begun to prop themselves as comfortably as possible. As they settled in for the night, none had any clue that they were being watched. From what used to be the center of the town stood an old bell tower. The tower was a perfect square building which rose into the air, not far enough to create an entire view of the city but high enough one could see many of the once busy roads through out. At the top of the tower were four wooden posts that supported a large wooden shingled roof which formed a perfect triangle. From this roof, two large cables suspended a large bell made of copper. From the night light one could see the engraving of a four legged horse like Tormite, who once lived in Tormor.

The night light also created shadows under the large roof. It is from these shadows that a small figure stirred. This creature could not be seen entirely but the outline was that of a small worf. It was Grainger who stood in the shadows and starred at the intruders to the city that he had claimed as his own. He leaned towards and put his hands on one of the posts which aloud the night light to shine upon them. His eye became reflective so close the light as well.

“So, the one who takes my information dares to reenter my Tormor,” Grainger said to himself. “He promised to leave Tormor solely to me.”

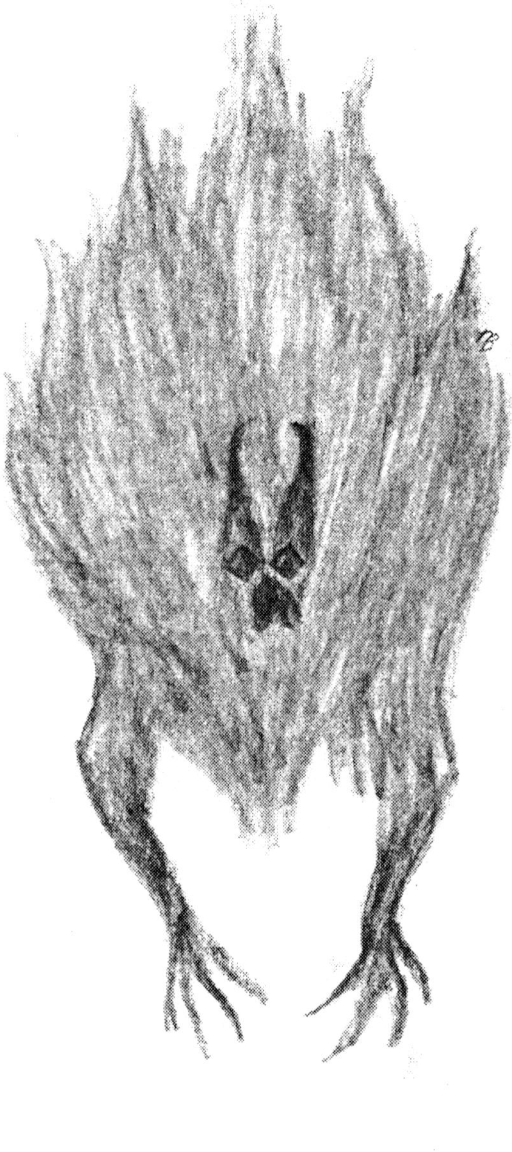

Grainger pulled himself away from the nightlight and stood for a moment in the darkness of the shadows.

"And now he returns here with and army," he continues. "Come here to take Tormor away from me, I don't think so. Make him regret that decision I will."

Grainger then ran through the shadows towards the center of the bell tower, where just under the bell was an opening with a long wooden ladder to the ground. Grainger jumped onto the ladder, briefly being visible by the night light. He slid silently down the side of the ladder to the bottom of the tower. He then disappeared into the shadows of the ruins structures of Tormor.

As Grainger disappeared, Captain Crig approached a small wooden hut that was completely untouched by all of the devastation surrounding it. The captain walked up to the door and knocked.

"You may enter Captain," The mysterious leader said from inside.

Captain Crig entered the hut to find a comfortable fire in the cobblestone fireplace and tranquil atmosphere. He walked up to the fire which blocked view of the leader.

"Sir, the troops have settled for the night, I have placed some to stand post in shifts until the return of the skylight," Captain Crig explained.

"Wonderful news Captain, thank you," the leader said. "You shall find suitable shelter for the night close by, for now that is all."

"Yes sir," Crig said as he turned and walked back out the door into the night.

From behind the fire a piece of the stone being held by the unseen leader glowed in the direction of Artonia.

"Now why are you pointing me in the opposite direction of which I wish to travel?" The leader asked himself, "What are to telling me?"

The leader fell silent for a moment. Then came a gentle breath.

"I shall have to find out what you are trying to tell me," he said. "But first we shall continue onward for my answers."

As an unknown trouble began to brew in Tormor, Marky, Slash and Levy had followed Polar back to his home and were saying there goodbyes at the door.

"Well, thank you very much for all that you have done," Marky said.

"Just doing what I felt to be the right thing to do," Polar replied.

"It has been most helpful just the same," Levy explained. "Finding this piece of the stone would not have been as easy if it were not for your help."

Polar smiled with pride. As light snow began to fall Marky, Slash and Levy decided to be off.

"Well, we had best be going if we are to be there by the light," Slash said.

"Oh wait just a minute," Polar said as he opened the door and walked into this home. "I have something for you," he hollered from inside.

As the candle light inside the home burned it was very dark outside, for the slow falling snow soaked up the night light. Enough light did shine through the window and opened door to show Marky, Slash and Levy standing close to each other at the foot of the threshold. Polar came back outside holding a large hide which once covered the body of a Terrance Hound.

"When you reach Zim's he will most likely expect a trade for the stone," Polar said. "This hide should be more than appealing to him enough to make the trade, especially since he has been forced to hold onto it for so many years."

Polar then leaned towards Marky and wrapped the arms of the hide around his neck, tight enough so not to fall off.

"There," he said. "That should hold on tightly enough to make it to Zim's"

"Quite warm as well," Marky replied.

"Terrance Hound hide is the warmest hide to have," Polar said. "Now we aren't to hunt them any longer and that is why I feel that it will be of great trade use for you."

Polar then noticed Chill on the inside leaning against the brown stained window.

"I believe my son wish you off in good luck as well," he said.

As Marky, Slash and Levy looked into the window; Chill waved his right hand to them and smiled.

"Well we should be off," Levy said. "Until we meet again!"

As they began to walk away they each waved at Chill on the other side of the window. They would not walk far before they became engulfed by the snowy night. Chill rushed to the door and stood by his father.

"Father, did they take the stone?" He asked.

"Yes they did," Polar answered.

"Wow, they bust be brave to take the stone one their own," Chill said.

"I believe that they are in fact very brave," Polar said. "Come let us go inside before we become too cold," Polar said.

Polar placed his arm around his son and they went back inside the dwelling and close the door behind them.

As Marky, Slash and Levy began their trek into the dark snowy night in the Artic Region; Kelso sat awake on top of a plateau in the Godway Region staring at the fire burning in the center. Nelty awoke from his sleep to notice Kelso who seemed to have a look of confidence on his face. This made Nelty quite curious.

"I was just telling myself, 'Nelty that one sure looks confident,'" Nelty said with a yawn at the end of his sentence.

"I apologize," Kelso said. "Did I wake you from your sleep?" he asked.

"Oh no you did no such thing, after my long sleep in the recent past I feel the urge only to nap from here to there," Nelty replied.

Kelso turned his head from Nelty back into the fire. Nelty sat up and too began to glance into it as well. Nelty pulled his head back away from the fire long enough to observe Crete curled into his rock formation for sleep. He glanced at Randor who was deeply rooted into the rock fast asleep with his sparsely scattered leaves blowing in the night breeze. Between Randor and Kelso slept Reamy who, unlike most bats, slept standing up in the wind with his wings acting as supports.

"Now why has such a look crossed your face?" Nelty asked as he turned his head towards Kelso. "Is it not rare to see such a look of confidence on a Powder Trolls Face?"

"For a Powder Troll to show the look of confidence in front of any other creature is feared to bring on aggravated attacks," Kelso said. "But after your descriptions of the Chosen Ones, as I know them, I can not help but feel pride in what they are doing, I feel confident that they will succeed, as will we."

"Well, rest assured that we need all of the confidence that we can muster," Reamy said opening one eye towards Nelty and Kelso.

"Did we wake you? Kelso asked.

"Do not worry about that," Reamy said. "Just remember that no aggravated attacks shall come from anyone with whom you share this fire with," he said, closing his eye shut and again falling asleep.

"Do not believe that I will sleep much from know until the rise of the skylight," Kelso said to Nelty. "Please do not mind me."

"No worry, I believe that I too will give the fire some company until first light as well if you do not mind," Nelty said.

"No, please do so," Kelso replied.\

Randor and Crete remained asleep while Kelso and Nelty continued to stare at the fire. As the fire burned it created a dancing image in the reflective glaze of their eyes. The night sky lit up with many bright stars and moons and galaxies far away making for a spectacular view from the Godway Region.

As Darkness loomed over the Kelso and Nelty, so did it loom over the ruins of Tormor. With many of the Mirrormite Army asleep and a scattered handful standing guard at many of the sparse fires footprints of the invisible Grainger could be seen slowly making the way through the bodies. The mirrormite soldiers snored heavily and many turned with restlessness. Still Grainger moved through the army with no sound and with invisibility, no chance of being seen. Then his footprints stopped next to a solider who turned to his side and rubbed up against him. The solider opened his black eyes to sudden touch. He quickly raised himself up with a labored breath. He stared around to notice that nothing was near. He panned his head around to see nothing but resting soldiers lying about. Then the sound of dust being stirred up came into hearing distance. The solider looked down to the ground to notice the imprints of Grainger's footprints in the dusty road beneath him. Then, from out of no where, Grainger appeared in front of the soldier. The mirrormite momentarily stood in shock of Grainger but quickly yelled for help.

"Intruder in the camp," He shouted.

This woke many of the other troops who quickly rose to their feet ready for battle. Grainger looked at the soldier and smiled a most devious smile with his green teeth showing through. He then touched the mirrormite solider on the right leg, as he did so the leg of the solider began to slowly disappear. Grainger then disappeared from sight. In a short amount of time all but the head of the solider, the solider mumbled in anger as his head and voice disappeared from existence.

Many of the troops who had seen this attack circled aimlessly looked for the invisible assailant. Then just a few feet away from the first attack another soldier noticed the footprints.

"Here, he is here," said the solider.

The solider drew his jagged and rusty sword for confrontation, however before the sword was draw fully over the soldiers head, and invisible touch grasped the solider by the hip. In a short amount of time this solider too was lost forever. A solider standing next to the attack knocked over the fire burning beside him, the flames blew past Grainger and for only a moment, the fire showed the invisible attacker. The fire then went out as so did Grainger's brief visibility.

"What is going on here?" Captain Crig said as he parted his way through his men.

"Sir," yelled a solider that came running up to the captain and grasped him by the shoulder. "An invisible creature is attacking our troops."

The solider then pointed to were the Captain could see his troops by the dozens now beginning to disappear.

"What is this?" the Captain asked.

Then the invisible touch of Grainger reached the soldier next to Crig. From the waste line, the solider began to disappear. Captain Crig quickly removed himself from contact with the soldier and watched as the solider disappeared from his sight. This prompted the captain to make hast towards the hut of the leader. He opened the door to find the unseen leader standing in the shadows hidden from sight. He was by the window observing the attack.

"I thought that this place was safe?" Captain Crig said to the leader.

"Perhaps my informant mistakes our intentions here in Tormor," the leader said.

He then peered through the open framed window to see many more of the troops disappearing into nothing. Captain Crig stood quite impatient, breathing heavily.

"Captain, tell your troops to fall out of the city, we shall begin our march again," the leader said. "I suggest you make haste as well."

"But what about this invisible intruder?" Captain Crig asked.

"Captain I recommend that you pull the army out of the city at once or there will be no army left to do anything," the leader responded.

Crig stormed back into the fray as soldiers around him disappeared.

"Reform your posts and fall out of the city by means of the south road," he said. "Pull out by means of the south road at once."

As the Mirrormite Army made hast to the city boundary the unseen leader looked from inside the shadows of the hut to notice the footprints on the ground then a soldier beside them disappeared. Grainger soon appeared from invisibility and stared into the shadow of the hut.

"Leave now, this is my Tormor," he hollered.

Grainger then fled out of sight and vanished from the attack site completely. As the skylight began to rise the Mirrormite Army could be seen marching away into the remaining darkness as if nothing had happen. Grainger stood in the bell tower jumping and laughing a cackled laugh.

"Tormor is mine, Tormor is mine," he said.

As the Mirrormite Army disappeared into the dark horizon, a bright horizon had snuck in on and past Marky, Slash and Levy. They were now inside the Cold Climate region and had begun to realize how it had gotten its name. The cold Climate Region was very snowy and bitterly cold. Soft rolling hills covered the landscape with white powder snow to boot. The bitter cold however did make it difficult on the three friends. Slash and Levy were quite worn down due to the cold while Marky, who was kept warmer by the hide on his back, was slowed greatly by its weight which pushed him farther down into the snow.

"Are you alright?" Levy asked Marky.

"Yes," Marky said struggling to make it onward.

"The hide looks to be freezing a little, is it making it heavier?" Slash asked.

"Very much," Marky replied.

"Shall we help you carry it?" Slash asked.

"I appreciate it but we are all equally worn thin as it is," Marky replied. "I fear it will only slow us down even further."

They pressed on into the snowstorm with no intention of stopping. Cold and worn of strength, they had realized that they were now beginning to wear severely. At the top of a small hill side, Marky stopped.

"What is wrong?" Slash asked.

"Slowly I have become so strained," Marky said.

"The Soul Dust has worn of us," Levy said. "That can be the only reason."

"I too feel quite weak," Slash said. "Let us all share the burden of the hide."

"I can make it further," Marky said weakly.

Marky began to take one step forward down the hill side. But another would not be. He stumbled to the ground and slide to the bottom of the hill.

"Marky," Levy shouted.

"Marky," Slash repeated immediately after Levy.

Marky lay at the bottom of the hill with no movement to show his friends. Slash and Levy stood worried at the top of the hill.

They began to run down the hill side towards their fallen friend. As they gained on Marky, Slash began to slow down and fall behind.

"I feel so weak," he said to Levy. "I can't stop."

With thoughts words said, Slash fell face first into the snow and slide the last half of the way down. He stopped only when colliding with Marky's motionless body. Levy reached the bottom of the hill and approached his friends. He could not believe how powerful the Soul dust had been and that his friends had fallen unwillingly.

"We can't stop," he said to himself. "We can make it onward."

However, Levy had begun to close his eyes. As he turned his head sideways, he fell with uncontrolled abandonment and slammed into the powdery snow, this created a large cloud of snow which quickly disappeared in the snowstorm. Marky, Slash and Levy lay helpless in the cold with no known hope in sight.

Miles away from the Cold Climate Region inside the Godway Region, Randor and Crete stood at the south end of the Boundary River. The rustling river looked quite different farther south than it had when Marky, Slash and Levy had to cross it. There would be no bridge to cross at this ford though. With Kelso and Nelty on board Randor began his move across the river.

"Climb high my friends, I do not wish to see the Brown Pike knock you into the water," Randor said. "That would be a most unfortunate end."

Kelso and Nelty climbed high into Randor's canopy. As Randor entered further into the Boundary River the water clearly was becoming deeper. Randor moved as quickly as possible but the force of the combining smooth and fierce currents from up north were making it a slow process.

"I believe that we are sinking further into the river, are we not?" asked Nelty.

"Do not worry," said Randor. "You shall make it from where you are."

Then from out of nowhere, the Brown Pike had begun to shoot out of the water and attack Randor just as they had attacked Marky, Slash and Levy at Cretan Bridge. The large brown fish jumped quite high but were unable to reach Kelso and Nelty. Half way through the river Randor himself was under water. All but the tops of his canopy were above water. The Brown Pike were very close to reaching Kelso and Nelty who had become almost sitting targets. Just when it had seemed that the flopping and bouncing fish were sure to hit them and knock them into the water below, Randor began to reemerge from the water.

From other side of the river stood Crete with Reamy perched on his right shoulder. They had been observing the incident before crossing.

"I am afraid that you will have to fly across the river, for I am not as tall as Randor," Crete said to Reamy.

"Alright," Reamy replied. "See you on the other side."

Reamy flew across the river and met Randor, Kelso and Nelty on the other side. They stood by as they watched Crete plunge step by step into the waters. Being as big as he was, he did not move as quickly under water. The Brown Pike hit him fiercely which made little impact on the giant. Soon Crete disappeared completely under water. Although out of sight, the sound of Crete pounding the river floor could be heard and felt as well. The current of the river had returned to normal giving no clues as to what was underneath. As Reamy landed next to Kelso and Nelty, the four watched the bank line for their fifth friend. Then with a large splash Crete rose from the water and walked onto the shore. The water ran off of him like a giant waterfall. He stretched and smiled.

"It has been quite some time since I have had the pleasure of being covered with water," he said. "It is most refreshing."

"It has been some time for me as well," Kelso said. "I wish I could have felt that."

Crete leaded over to the river and scooped up a handful of water. He straightened up and effortlessly through the water and tossed it towards Kelso, splashing him as well as Reamy and Nelty. The water splashed to the ground.

"Well, I was just thinking, I didn't need the bath but thank you anyway," A drenched Nelty said spitting water from his mouth.

Reamy stood shaking himself as he too was engulfed with water. Kelso shook himself off with a slight smile upon his face.

"That was the most superb washing that I have had for much a long time," Kelso complimented. "I feel quite refreshed myself."

"How about you Randor?" asked Reamy.

I have never yet complained about water in any form," he replied politely. "In fact I believe that the water has come in quite nicely before we reach the land of Hyden."

"Hmmm, land of the tall trees," Crete said.

"Yes, much taller than I," Randor replied.

"Very muggy if you ask me," Reamy said.

"Yes, but not as hot nor dry as our destination," Randor replied. "This is what we proceed to now. We will follow the Boundary River into the Desert Location."

Walking away refreshed from a simple rinse, Randor, Crete, Reamy, Nelty and Kelso entered the land of Hyden. The land of the 'tall trees' as Crete called it dwarfed the giant and towering statures of Randor and Crete as they began to follow the river.

Chapter 11

Bucket Ride

Marky, Slash and Levy now laid together on a cobblestone floor, out cold and unconscious. In the background a small furry white chiller stood next to a gray haired chiller. They appeared to be cooking something over a cast iron stove with blue flames coming from the burners. With pots and pans hanging about the home was cluttered but cozy.

"Now mother," said the gray haired chiller. "Not too much cobble root now, or you will make them to hyper."

"Now father, I can remember," the white chiller replied, "Just because I have not made this for a while, does not label me forgetful."

In front of the old couple was a small pot with copper handles placed on the corner burner. Inside was a pink soupy fluid that bubbled with heat.

"Now father, turn the fire off," said the white Chiller.

The white chiller poured the fluid into a thin bottle and passed it the gray chiller beside her. The gray chiller walked over to a thick wooden table and placed the bottle near the edge. He then grabbed a small burlap bag and placed his hand inside as he walked to the table. He placed the bag next to the bottle with the pink soupy fluid. He pulled out his hand which held a sparkling white powder which poured through his furry gray fingertips. He placed his hand over the bottle and released the sparkling powder. Most of the powder fell into the bottle causing the fluid to turn into a sparkling pink powder. Then came a lid with large holes in the top.

"There mother, I believe we have it," said the gray chiller.

"Let us hope there is time left," said the white chiller.

They both walked over to Marky, Slash and Levy, the white chiller stood by Marky, while the gray chiller covered the three friends with the pink powder by shaking it over them. He shook the bottle until the powder was gone from the bottle.

"That is the jest of it mother," said the gray chiller as he and the white chiller backed away from Marky, Slash and Levy. "We simply stand here and wait," he said.

The pink powder sparkled as it disappeared. The white and gray chiller stood by; with wire rim spectacles on their little noses they watched. In a split second, Marky, Slash and Levy opened their eyes and stood up coughing. The chillers embraced each other with delight.

"Where are we?" Levy asked while looking around coughing.

"Oh please do not worry," said the gray chiller. "You are safe in our home."

"But where is that exactly," Marky asked.

"You're at the center of the Cold Climate Region," said the white chiller.

The three friends continued to cough as they gained their bearings.

"I apologize for the coughing, but the Revitalization Powder enters the mouths as well as the skin and the remains must be coughed clean," the gray chiller said.

"Powder," Slash questioned.

"Forgive me for my manners," said the gray chiller. "You were all but dead, it appeared that you had once had soul dust in your system, unfortunately when it finally worn off the cold weather put your bodies in a state of reversal shock."

"I apologize myself but I do not understand," said Levy.

"You see," said the gray chiller sitting down at his table. "When soul dust eventually fades away your bodies would return to normal wear and tear, however, it is my belief that what ever drove you out this far into the Cold Climate Region had you so distressed that when the powder wore off, your strain caught up with you, and instead of returning to normal, your bodies simply passed out."

Marky, Slash and Levy stood understanding what was told to them and appeared to be most grateful for the treatment they had received.

"But how did we come to be here," Slash asked.

"I was returning from one of my daily trades when I came across you three lying in the powder almost covered," the gray chiller said placing his furry arms onto the table as the white chiller sat down beside him. "I place you three on my cart and brought you home so that we would have a chance to save you if possible."

Just then a small steam whistle blew by the stove. The white chiller stood up and made her way over and uncovered a large pan of freshly made bread.

"Now you young lad's best eat, I am sure you are hungry," she said bringing the pan over to the table and sitting back down.

"Please come and eat and tell us why you are this far north in Mavenwood," the gray chiller said as he grabbed a freshly cut slice of the bread.

"Thank you very much," Levy said as him and his friends sat down to the table.

"Are you lads warm enough," asked the white chiller.

"Very fine thank you," Marky replied.

"Well dig in, dig in," said the gray chiller.

Marky, Slash and Levy began to eat the bread placed on their plates before them by the very kind white chiller. Even though they were in fact very hungry, they eat with poise and manners as they had always been taught to before others.

"Now say," said the gray chiller. "What has brought you out so far from anything else? I have never seen creatures like yourselves before, but then again there are parts of Mavenwood that I have not traded in just yet."

"Well sir," said Levy. "We have come looking for a chiller who is said to have something that we so gravely must have."

"And what just might that be, if I many ask," asked the gray chiller.

"We are looking for a stone, well actually part of a stone," Levy continued.

"You don't say," said the gray chiller as he ate. "I've seen many stones in my time. What does it look like," he asked.

"We aren't sure really," Slash answered. "Some of the pieces we have retrieved before look different than their siblings. It would be sandy colored, and have very rough edges as if broken away from other stones."

"It might have drawings or words on it, we are not sure," Marky added.

"Well then maybe we if you tell us who you seek we can tell you where they are," said the white chiller. "We are a spread out civilization but we know many others too."

"We are looking for a chiller they call Zim," Levy said.

The chillers stopped eating and look surprised.

"Have we said something wrong," Levy asked.

"Oh no, no," said the gray chiller slightly laughing as he sat his bread down. "It is most entertaining that I should find you three then."

"You mean," Marky said.

"Yes, I am Zim," said the gray chiller. "And this is my wife Zoe."

"Most nice to meet you," said Zoe.

"What stone is it that I posses that you wish to have," Zim asked. "I have many stones lust lying about around here."

"High Priest Frost from Artonia had told us that you once tried to trade it for goods a long, long time ago," Levy stated.

Zim sat in tough for a moment before widening his eyes.

"Yes, the cruddy old sandstone I found not far from here," Zim said. "I had much trouble try to off load it."

"Can you take us to it," Marky asked.

"Yes, yes follow me," Zim said.

Zim and his wife stood up and walked over to a small door with a red dusty curtain over it. Marky, Slash and Levy approached the door as Zim grabbed the curtain.

"It is in here," he said.

Zim drew back the curtain and walked inside a room that was lit by a single large burning candle stuck in a holder on the wall next to the doorway. Inside were many shelves with different stones and gems gathered from other regions of Mavenwood. Marky, Slash and Levy entered to find Zoe standing beside the candle, watching Zim thumb up and down the shelving.

"No, no that isn't it either," Zim said.

"I'm sorry but it is not on that side of the room," Slash said.

"Where is it," Marky asked.

"Over there," Slash answered nudging his head to the opposite end of the room.

Levy walked over towards the stone covered shelves and looked. As he looked to the floor, he noticed a stone that was covered with dust, he judged it gently. As some of the dust fell away the stone had a soft glow to it, he pulled the stone out from under the bottom shelf. The glowing stone attracted all who were inside the room. Slash began to feel the pressure of the stone against his chest.

"This is the stone, I know it," he told Marky as they walked up to Levy.

Levy stood back as Slash approached the dusty old stone.

The Stone began to glow brightly as it turned to gold powder and was absorbed by the orb around Slash's chest. The increase of matter in the orb began to weigh more heavily on Slash. He stretched his neck before adjusting to the new weight.

"It's becoming heavier," Marky said.

"A little, but still not that terrible," Slash replied. "I just have to adjust my neck."

"Umm, I don't mean to sound cold, but can there be a trade from you three for that stone," Zim asked. "I was sure I would never trade it to anyone, but we would like to make this exchange even."

"That is right," Marky said. "I almost forgot."

Marky left the room, only to return with the Terrance Hound hide that was given to him when he, Slash and Levy were in Artonia.

"I apologize, but this had completely slipped out of my mind," he said to Zim.

Marky approached Zim and laid before him the hide that had been on his back.

"I do believe that is Terrance Hound hide, is it not," Zim asked.

"Yes," Marky answered. "A friend of ours from the Artic Region said that it might of worth to you in return for the stone."

Zim smiled and opened his widely as he began dance in a circle clapping his hands. His happiness surprised the three friends as did it surprise Zoe.

"I accept the trade, thank you with very much appreciation," Zim said. "Hide is not available since hunting the Terrance Hounds is no long accepted." Zim then grasped the hide close to him, "A most wonderful trade."

"Well, now that that is done," Zoe said. "Would you like to stay for a bit," She asked.

Marky, Slash and Levy looked at each other wishing they could stay and visit with their two newest friends but knew that their journey could not rest until all of the stone were retrieved and safe from danger.

"We are sorry but we must go for now," Levy said with a gentle smile.

"Where will you three be off to now," Zim asked.

"I believe that we should return to Randor with what we have and know," Levy said looking to Marky and Slash.

"I agree, we are still worn over and the orb is beginning to become a labor," Marky stated as he looked to Slash, who with a look on his face agreed about the strain that was growing upon him now.

"That is alright with me, at least the stones we have will be safe with Randor," Slash said. "Safer than with me right now."

"Randor you say," asked Zim. "Then you will be returning to the Woods of Syrus will you not." he asked again with a sparkle in his eye.

"Yes that is right," Slash answered.

"Can you help us return there," Levy asked.

"Well, yes in a round about sort of way," Zim replied. "My way will not take you directly to the Woods of Syrus but it will cut down on the days you will lose by walking."

"How would we be getting there," Marky asked.

"Follow me," Zim said as he walked by Marky, Slash and Levy waving his hand.

Zim had taken the three outside and up to a mountain that was off in the distance from his home. At this time of day, the snowfall had stopped and the skylight was shining brightly. The five creatures stood at the base of the small mountain and stared at an amazing and awkward contraption.

"My friends, I give you," Zim said rising is hand up at the mountain, "The Railway. Only one of a kind," he added.

As Marky, Slash and Levy looked up the mountain they could see a wooden shack with a slanted roof over it. From the shack emerged a massive metal rail that along with many sets of stilts to hold it up span outward and as Marky, Slash and Levy soon realized run behind Zim's cozy home and off as far as their eyes could see.

"Wow, that is quite a spectacle," Slash remarked.

"Oh, please most others could care less about it," Zim said.

Zim noticed an interested look on the faces of Marky, Slash and Levy as they peered at the Railway as if they had never seen anything like it before.

"Say, let me take you three closer," Zim said with a smile.

They climbed the snow covered mountain and entered the shanty shack. Inside was the end of the railway. A large wooden basket was hooked to the railway, the bucket, which was larger than any that Marky, Slash and Levy had ever seen back home, looked almost as old at the shack covering it.

"And what will this do for us," Marky asked.

"Well," Zim replied. "If you are wishing to return to the Woods of Syrus this will help you by quickly getting you one third the way much fast than walking it. Of course it will take you not directly in the right direction," he added.

"How will it take us," Levy questioned.

"Well it will take you through the Lynden Mountains and over the Malloy Dessert before ending south of the dessert inside the land of Hyden," Zim answered. From there, it will only be a hop through Mortere Prairie, a skip through the corner of the Land of the Rock Gods and a jump into the Woods of Syrus."

"Well," asked Marky. "How do we use it."

"Well just climb inside first," Zim requested.

Zim climbed a ladder and grabbed the edge of the large bucket. He then jumped off of the ladder and pulled the bucket over on its hinges down so that Marky, Slash and Levy could walk into it. The three stood quite worried about this.

"Now don't you be afraid," said Zoe. "You can trust in the railway."

Marky, Slash and Levy entered the bucket. Zim let go of the edge to let the bucket spring back to its original place. Zim then walked over to a small bench at the back of the shack where a dozen rusted cans were placed.

"Now which one is it," he asked himself aloud.

Then he reached inside a can and pulled out what appeared to be dirt. With a smile on his face, climbed the ladder once again to the top this time where a large metal lever was connected. He recklessly tossed the can into the bucket.

"Now remember when you get out of the bucket, kindly through some of this return mineral onto the pulleys so that it will return to the shack," Zim instructed. "I would like to use it without having to first fetch it on foot."

With things moving slightly fast for the three friends, Marky, Slash and Levy could not help but look unsure about everything.

"I'm sorry but I have a question about the dirt," Slash said.

"Good luck," Zim said as he pulled down the lever releasing the bucket and sending it speeding down the mountain side on the rail.

Marky, Slash and Levy had wide eyes as they made the drop down out of the shack. Soon the railway straightened out and the three looked out from the top to see the shack becoming smaller and smaller at a rapid pace.

"Wow, he wasn't joking about the speed," Marky said as he turned his head to the front of the bucket. "I can't believe it."

Marky, Slash and Levy moved quite quickly as The Railway carried them to the edge of the Cold Climate Region and into the sliver of land jutting up from the Land of Nothing. The three looked to see the snowy mountains give way to the pink leafed Dwarfwood Trees which covered the Land of Nothing. The once white and cold landscape had giving way to growing red berries on the thousands upon thousands of trees grown across the land. They also noticed the droves of Powder Trolls like Kelso, picking the red berries from the Dwarfwood Trees and placing them inside whicker baskets.

"Look," Marky said nudging his head forward.

Slash and Levy looked ahead to notice a colossal set of mountains.

"That must be the beginning of the Lynden Mountains," Levy said.

The Railway led them straight into the sky scraping mountains and made bends and curves as it stretched its way through. Marky, Slash and Levy were in shock of how massive the landmarks were that covered the ground. Slash peered down to the bottom to notice how far off of the ground they were.

"Wow," he said. "I've never been this high off of anything before."

Marky and Levy took a gaze over the side and grew wide eyes at the height, for they were at least one hundreds stories up into the air. The three ducked back inside the bucket away from the view.

"Very high," Marky sighed.

Levy shook his head in agreement. But inside their heads they each knew that this was simply another branch of their journey which had to be taken for the safety of Mavenwood and the safe return of the stones. They continued onward into the Lynden Mountains as The Mirrormite Army entered the land of Hyden in full force, and as Randor, Crete, Reamy, Nelty and Kelso continued to follow the Boundary River towards the boundary of Hyden with the Desert Location.

As the night light took control of the sky, Marky, Slash and Levy had fallen asleep inside the large bucket. Then suddenly without warning, were awoken to a loud thud against the bucket.

"What was that," asked Marky.

Levy stood to look outside as a large rock rolled down the mountain and slammed into them knocking him back down.

"It is a rock slide," Levy answered. "It's rolling down towards us."

After a close encounter with yet another rock, it was clear that the bucket could not handle repeated collisions without possibly being knocked away from the rail. The three friends stood and watched the mountain side and could see the falling rocks in the night light for a good distance ahead. Levy looked to the pulleys above him and had and idea as to possibly moving the bucket away from the falling rocks.

"When they get close to us, we are going to have to move the bucket away from the mountain side so that the rocks can pass without harm," he said.

"But how," asked Slash.

"We put our combined force against the bucket," Levy replied. "Those pulleys look to have a hinge on them, if we can use our weight to move the bucket, we can miss the rocks, and it is our only chance."

"We have to try then, we might not be able to stand to many more hits like the first one," Marky said. "It's worth a good try."

Being that they were moving so fast, it was hard to judge the falling rocks. Their first attempt was a miscue which knocked them right back into the bucket. They each rose and watched as they were coming up fast upon a large rock that looked to make a collision.

"Ready," asked Levy. "We are going to have to time this just right."

"Ready," Slash replied. "Holler when its time."

"We'll give it all that we have," Marky said.

As the rock barreled down the mountain side, Marky, Slash and Levy drew closer.

As they approached the target with the rock, Levy hollered and the three friends pushed up against the side of the bucket, and just as they had hoped, the bucket swung outwards and missed what could have been a deadly impact. Then, without any moment to rest, another rock, not as large though, came crashing down and again the three had to muster the force to push against the bucket to make it move.

"That was close on that one," Slash said.

"Almost to close," answered Marky.

"Here comes another one," Levy warned. "Get ready."

Again and for the next few miles, they swung the bucket safely from danger. But soon they would pass the avalanche and fine calm sailing through the rest of the Lynden Mountains. After absorbing the view for quite some time the three friends decided to lie in the bucket for a sleep until the end of the railway drew near.

As the skylight rose from the horizon, the railway had carried Marky, Slash and Levy into the familiar white sands of the Malloy Desert. The sands glittered like shooting stars across the ground. Now the Railway had the three now more that forty stores in the air. It would take not one quarter of the day to cross the desert and enter the land of Hyden. As Marky, Slash and Levy laid peacefully the bucket made a sudden stop which jerked the three around and woke them from sleep. Fully rested, they stood up, just then the pulley system pivoted and the bucket tipped over and the three friends fell out of the bucket. Quickly to there feet, they each stared in separate directions with the look of grim surprise on their faces.

"Of any place in Hyden we would have to land, it would be here," Marky said.

For luck had turned against them this time. The railway had end right in the middle of the Mirrormite Army. The army was already alerted with the thump the railway made at its ending. From out of within the army Captain Crig's voice could be heard.

"All right out of the way," said the captain. "What is it," he asked.

The captain emerged from his troops to lay eyes upon Marky, Slash and Levy. As the solid structure of Captain Crig stood before them, an evil smile grew across his face.

"Well, well what is before us now," he asked. "I looks like three creatures that I have been so warned about."

Marky, Slash and Levy said nothing but there positive expressions told enough that they were not afraid of there sudden misfortune.

"The leader is on his way, he will be most pleased to find that you have found him," Captain Crig explained. "Most pleased!"

Inside the army, a soldiers voice could be heard, "Make way for the leader," he said. Flight by flight, the troops made an isle for the leader to ride his black Scrownge across as he headed towards his captain. The army fell back into rank as he past them one by one. The heavy breathing of the Scrownge could be heard through the silence which lingered under the canopy of the enormously tall trees of Hyden. The unseen leader approached the center where Marky, Slash and Levy stood along side the railway with the look of determination for what ever was to happen.

The leader approached Marky, Slash and Levy and turned his trusted steed to the side so to have a better view of the ones he had been searching for. Marky, Slash and Levy stood in puzzlement before realizing who the unseen leader was, there faces then were that of shock and wonder.

"We have seen your face before haven't we," asked Levy.

"Once before, yes," said the leader. "But I have seen your faces many times, only one moment other than this has peaked my curiosity this much though."

"And which moment is that," asked Marky.

"When you defeated my master at the top of the Tower of Maytane," said the leader. "You three where most impressive, but story has it that you three were also nearly destroyed as well, thank goodness for the River of Guidance, no," he asked.

"Yes, you were the frightened one who took off down the staircase were you not," Slash asked. "That was you."

"My name is Quaker," said the now seen leader.

The leader was one time aid to Zytor, Quaker, who almost took a striking resemblance to Zim from the Cold Climate Region. This time the once shaken body had become steady and confident. The one time look of fear was replaced with a domineer of confidence and resolve.

"It is amazing what a little stone can do to ones self esteem," said Quaker, who stepped off of his Scrownge walked towards Slash. "But then again you already know that don't you," he asked while staring at the orb around Slash's chest.

Quaker snapped his fingers and two soldiers stepped out from the army and opened a satchel draped over the hide end of the Scrownge and pulled out the peace of stone that Quaker had in his possession. The soldiers walked over to Quaker and handed him the stone and turned and rejoined their flight. The stone glowed and began to shake the closer Quaker walked towards Slash, Slash's orb too began to glow bright white with the last piece of stone drawing near.

"You see my master too was not always so feared but when he found this stone he also felt the incredible power of it," Quaker said.

"Only he did not plan on us stopping him," Marky said in a strong tone of voice.

"No, that was a minor setback of course," Quaker said. "You defeated a force so grand that many thought that it could never be stopped. But I on the other hand will not make the same mistake as he."

Quaker stopped and placed his stone on the ground before him. As the hot winds of Hyden blew under the tall trees Quaker stood away from it and pointed at Slash's orb.

"Now then, release the stones and let this journey come to an end," Quaker said.

"And if we do not," asked Levy turning his head to the side in defiance.

The Mirrormite Army closed the circle around them tighter.

"You can here by means of that," Quaker asked of the Railway. "Perhaps even this old contraption is worth a look at."

Marky noticed the can of return mineral lying at his feet. He quickly kicked the can with his front feet right at the pulleys of the railway bucket. The dirt like mineral covered the pulleys, then without warning, the bucket made off like a bullet in the direction from which it had come.

"Well, perhaps not," Quaker said with a mad frown. "Now, give me the remaining pieces to the Stone of Afadavis."

Quaker looked at Slash and pointed to the ground before him. Slash took a deep breath and began to walk forward.

"No, we can't," Marky said.

"I don't think we have much choice," Slash said looking towards Levy.

Levy looked around and saw that there was no chance of an escape and with the size of the Mirrormite Army, he knew Slash was correct.

"Slash is right Marky," Levy whispered. "With any luck we might be able to find them again, if we can make it through this alive."

Marky reluctantly shook his head in agreement. Slash then walked looked down at Quakers stone lying on the ground. He then stared at the Randor and Gecko the Great had given him, he took a deep breath.

"Metamorphous Ra," he said.

Just as before the contents of the orb spilled out over the ground, only this time they were drawn directly onto the tabled placed by Quaker. When the dust had settled, a strong gust of wind blew through the land of Hyden, and when the wind was gone, the Stone of Afadavis was lying completely intact before Quaker's feet. Quaker and the entire Mirrormite Army stood in awe at the power which was before them. The stone was cover with the Airtime Language which was unreadable by anyone. However, Levy noticed a word on the stone which he remembered from Gecko the Great's Lair, the word was Treimel Hartis that knew to mean Doomsday Device.

The orb which had been around Slash's chest for so long now began to crack like brittle dried mud. As it crackled and popped the orb itself shattered. The harness fell to pieces and crashed to the ground as powder.

Quaker snapped his fingers and four guards approached the stone and carried it off into the army. Quaker grinned at his foes as he tilted his head sideways.

"Now what do I do with you," he asked.

Captain Crig pulled out his sword and came at Marky, Slash and Levy with it raised high over his head. "Kill them," he said.

As the captain reached Marky, Slash and Levy, Quaker ordered him to stop.

"I do not want their demise to be quick, rather I would like it to be slow," Quaker said. "I have a more appealing idea."

"And what would that be," asked Captain Crig.

After a deep breath Quaker replied, "Have your Sky Crossers take them into the Desert Location and drop them off. With no food or water they will wish for a quick death, do you not agree Captain Crig," he asked.

Captain Crig began to laugh a most evil chuckle; he picked up an ivory tusk from his side and blew on it. The sound was most bellowing through the tall trees. It would not be long before the Sky Crossers could be seen circling above the trees over Marky, Slash and Levy. Then they crashed through the canopy of the tall tree and shook the ground as they landed. Captain Crig walked over to the Sky Crosser who had battled with the "Chosen One's" previously and gave the orders.

"Take them into the Desert Location and dump them out," he commanded.

Quaker walked away from Marky, Slash and Levy and mounted his Scrownge once again. He sat and stared at the infamous trio.

"It is a pity that you have to lose this way," he said. "You have been quite the opponents over time. But it is time that evil triumphs over good."

The dragons under the Sky Crossers each reached towards Marky, Slash and Levy. With one effortless swipe, the three heroes were grabbed up like leaves in the breeze and carried high above the trees of Hyden. Once of above the trees, the wings of the dragons stretched far and wide as they began to flap their wings and make way for the Desert Location. In the air Marky, Slash and Levy struggled to free themselves but soon were too high to fall safely. The air rushing against their faces made it impossible to communicate to one another. All they could do was watch helplessly as they crossed the land not knowing what would happen to them.

It would take almost the entire day for the Sky Crossers to reach the Desert Location. Soon after there would be nothing to see but brown sand for as long as one could see. The sand created waves of heat which rose from the grounds and reached towards the sky. The Sky Crossers then swooped down towards the sands. The dragons drug their claws through the sand as they released their cargo. Marky, Slash and Levy were left rolling over and over several times before they were able to stop themselves. They each stood and watched the

Sky Crossers sail away into nothing with the dragons flapping their wings. They looked around to see nothing but sand and more sand.

"We can't stay here," Marky said.

"If Hyden is that way," Levy said pointing the way they had come from. "Then that way has to be towards the Woods of Syrus," he said pointing the other directions.

Levy then noticed Slash looking slightly down from the recent turn of events. He walked to him in an attempt to console him.

"There was nothing that could be done," he said. "We had to give up the stones in hopes of having a chance to regain them again."

"We will find them again," Marky assured. "We must find Randor first though."

Slash smiled, "Your right," he said. "Live to fight another day."

"That's right," Marky said smiling.

"And fight we shall," Levy said smiling also. "It will be dark soon, let's be moving on, perhaps we are not terribly far into the desert."

The three began their journey back towards the Woods of Syrus in hopes of leaving the desert sometime in the night. They walked and walked as the sky light escaped their sight. By the time the night light had caught up with them, Marky, Slash and Levy were climbing up the side of a large sand dune. Marky stopped suddenly.

"Do you smell that," Marky asked.

Levy and Slash also stopped and began smelling the night desert air.

"Smells like a fire," Slash said.

"Yes," Marky replied. "A campfire, someone is out their."

The three slowly reached the top of the dune and looked out across the desert. In complete shock they saw the very friends that they were returning to. Randor, Crete, Reamy, Nelty and Kelso were all gather around the fire in discussion.

"Randor and the others," Slash said.

"Hurry let us join them," Levy said.

Marky, Slash and Levy took of towards the fire. As they gained closer, Reamy's good sense of hearing locked in on them.

"Someone is coming towards us from the darkness," Reamy said.

The group turned as the footsteps in the sand grew closer and closer.

"Be ready for anything," Randor forewarned.

Suddenly Marky, Slash and Levy reached the light of the fire. The faces of Randor, Reamy and Nelty became filled with happiness to see their three friends who disappeared so long ago.

"Randor, it is our friends," Nelty said, who rushed out to meet them.

Nelty hugged each of his friends and danced in the sand with joy.

"We were afraid that we might never see you again," Randor said with a smile.

"I remember you three from a long time ago," Crete said shaking his head.

Randor then noticed that the orb was no longer around Slash's chest, his eyes widened with worry.

"We found out who was looking for the stone," Slash said.

"Randor, there is nothing that can be done through the night," Crete said.

"Come now," Randor said. "Sit around the fire and tell us everything that has happen since we parted ways."

Marky, Slash and Levy sat by the fire and told of the trouble on Sikes Bridge, and how they nearly escaped the Dark Valley. They told of the Terrance Hounds and the kindness of Polar and his son Chill as well as Zim and Zoe. Randor was surprised to hear to hear of how it was Quaker who was looking for the stones and how he had aligned with the Mirrormite Army.

Randor then told of their plans to go before the Collective Council and try to stop what was about to start. With the fire crackling, old friends became new again and what was once a strained struggle had now become as strong as it had ever been.